The End of Always

of

Always

Rebecca Phillips

Second Story Press

Library and Archives Canada Cataloguing in Publication

Title: The end of always / Rebecca Phillips.
Names: Phillips, Rebecca (Young adult author), author.
Identifiers: Canadiana (print) 20230515983 | Canadiana (ebook)
    20230515991 | ISBN 9781772603712 (softcover) | ISBN
    9781772603798 (EPUB)
Subjects: LCGFT: Novels.
Classification: LCC PS8631.H558 E53 2024 | DDC jC813/.6—dc23

Printed and bound in Canada

*Second Story Press gratefully acknowledges the support of the Ontario Arts
Council and the Canada Council for the Arts for our publishing program.
We acknowledge the financial support of the Government of Canada through
the Canada Book Fund.*

Published by
Second Story Press
20 Maud Street, Suite 401
Toronto, Ontario, Canada
M5V 2M5
www.secondstorypress.ca

"A fast-paced portrait of grief and growth, *The End of Always* illustrates the complexities of what happens to a family when a parent's societal fears shadow their children's lives. Thoughtful and moving, Phillips's narrative touches on themes of first love, sisterly bonds, and what it means to come of age."

—Joan F. Smith, author of *The Other Side of Infinity*

In loving memory of my dad, who is always with me

Chapter One

"Isobel."

The needle slips and pierces my skin. With a surprised yelp, I drop everything and stick my injured finger in my mouth, soothing the sting.

"Oh, crap, sorry," my father says from behind me. "I didn't mean to sneak up on you."

Finger still in my mouth, I turn to see him standing in the doorway to the kitchen, his black shirt covered in wood shavings. For a big guy, he moves around the house with the stealth and grace of a ninja.

"It's okay." I squint at the tiny red hole. "Not the first time I've stabbed myself with a beading needle."

My father, ever prepared, strides over to the first aid drawer for a Band-Aid and a tube of antibiotic cream. He places both beside me on the kitchen table, then peers at my latest project. "That's looking nice."

I shrug and pick up the half-finished crystal and pearl ladder wrap bracelet. The intricate design is tough, but I had a good rhythm going before Dad sprung up behind me. "Claire asked for a new one. Hopefully, the leather cord will hold this time." My best friend has broken or lost every piece of jewelry I've ever made her. Probably because she forgets to take stuff off before her games. At least three other bracelets are buried in the soccer field behind our high school.

Dad stands there for a moment, absently stroking his beard. There's a red mark on the bridge of his nose from his dust mask. He was woodworking in the garage—probably making more shelves for the basement—before he came to find me.

"Did you need me for something?" I ask, dotting some antibiotic cream on my fingertip. I do this for his sake. Unlike him, I'm not worried about infections or blood poisoning or any other condition that probably won't happen from a harmless little needlestick.

Dad blinks twice, like he's struggling to remember why he's standing in the kitchen with me. "Oh," he says. "Yes. I need you to watch April this afternoon. I have a meeting."

I wrap the Band-Aid around my finger, even though it's fine now. "On a Sunday?" My dad is an estimator for a real estate company that develops apartment buildings in the city, so he has meetings with construction people all the time. But not usually on the weekends. Saturdays and Sundays have always been for us—my sister April and me, and our mom when she was still alive.

Dad goes to the sink to wash his hands. "Not a work meeting," he says, his back to me. "There's a workshop at the community center. Intro to portable solar power."

I press my lips together and pick up my bracelet again. *Portable* solar power. Last year, he attached solar panels to the roof of the house, but even that's not enough for him anymore. Now he needs to know how to harness the sun *everywhere*. "I guess I can stick around," I say.

"Great." He dries his hands with a dish towel. "She's in the backyard with Rana. I'm gonna go grab a shower. Keep an eye on her, okay?"

"Okay," I say, even though I'm not worried about her playing in our fenced backyard. The kitchen window is open, so I can hear her giggling.

After he leaves, I go back to my bracelet. I'm almost finished by the time April bursts into the house, the screen door slamming shut behind her.

"Rana had to go home for dinner," she announces. Rana is her best friend...on our street. She has a dozen more best friends at school. "When are *we* eating? I'm hungry."

I look her over. She's red-cheeked and sweaty from running around beneath the warm May sun, her hair a tangled mess. I sigh. I'll be the one combing out those knots before her bath later because she hates the way Dad does it. She doesn't particularly like the way I do it either—Mom always had the magic touch with tangles. Probably because she had the same hair as April—thick and curly. Beautiful. I remember the day it started falling out during her chemo treatments. It was the first time I'd seen her cry over her cancer diagnosis, looking at that blond clump of hair in her hand.

I push away the memory and check my phone. It's almost five. Dad should be home soon.

"Well, then," I say, wiping a smudge of dirt off April's chin. "Let's start dinner."

Weekends are frozen food days in the McCarthy house. On weekdays, I usually throw together something involving some kind of vegetable, but on weekends, it's pizza or burgers or, when April gets her way, chicken nuggets. Today she gets her way.

"What do you want on the side?" I ask once the nuggets are in the oven.

She thinks about it for a minute. "Canned corn," she says. Her face lights up. "Can I get it by myself?"

"Sure."

She darts for the basement door. For some reason, she loves going down into Dad's storeroom, an eight-by-ten-foot space lined with custom shelves he built himself in the garage. One of Dad's hobbies is stocking up on whatever nonperishables are on sale. Three of the shelving units are stacked with food—cans and boxes and bags, enough to feed us for at least a year. The other shelf is for things like matches, lanterns, candles, and first aid items. The basement supplies aren't meant to be used, but Dad replaces whatever we take anyway.

The nuggets are half-done by the time she returns, canned corn in hand. "There are thirty-six cans of tomato soup," she tells me.

No wonder she took so long. "Wow. That's almost enough to fill up your pool."

She giggles, which turns into a cough. I frown. The basement dust isn't good for her allergies. "Are the chicken nuggets ready yet?"

"Almost."

I give her the job of gathering condiments and drinks while I take care of the corn. Dad gets home just as we sit down at the table.

"Hi, Daddy," April says as she dumps about half a cup of ketchup over her food. "We have thirty-six cans of tomato soup."

Dad goes over to the stove and plops a few chicken nuggets onto a plate. "Is that so? I'd better go shopping then."

April laughs: it doesn't take much to entertain a six-year-old.

"Sorry I'm late, girls," Dad says, sitting across from me. "I got talking to the guy who ran the workshop. He knows everything there is to know about solar power. There's this portable lithium power station that can keep all your devices and appliances charged for *days*."

"Why do we need that?" April asks. "We have power."

Dad's eyes gleam like they do whenever he's learned something new. I look away. "We have power right now, Sunshine, but there might come a day when we don't."

His nickname for her is so fitting. With her glossy hair and bright smile, she's like sunshine in little-girl form.

"Like when we had the hurricane?"

I raise my eyebrows, surprised she remembers. Two autumns ago, a couple of months after Mom died, we were hit with a Category Two hurricane that downed dozens of trees and knocked out power for days. Dad went a little bonkers securing the house beforehand, boarding up windows and hoarding packs of bottled water. During the worst of the storm, we hid out in the basement and played board games until the wind stopped shaking the house. In the end, the only damage we suffered was a broken lawn chair. For me, Dad's wild-eyed intensity was more memorable than the storm itself.

"Right, like the hurricane," he says. "Or something worse. You know, with climate change, extreme weather events are becoming more frequent and—"

"Dad," I cut in, "do you want some more corn?"

"You can eat as much as you want," April adds. "We have seventeen cans downstairs."

He looks at her, and I wonder if he's actually seeing her or imagining something else entirely. "We need to be ready," he says. It's like he didn't even hear us.

After dinner, Dad goes back to the garage while April and I make instant chocolate pudding for dessert. We take turns using the mixer, then I pour the finished pudding into dishes—I make an extra one for the two of us to share.

"Should we do whipped cream on top?" I ask.

April nods solemnly, like this is serious business, so I dig around for Mom's recipe book. She used to jot down recipes into a blue coil notebook, and I know there's one in there for a decadent, peanut butter–flavored whipped cream. We made it together once, for a chocolate pie.

I finally find the notebook in the cupboard above the fridge. My heart clenches a bit when I see Mom's neat printing. Almond tarts, tomato sauce, taco soup, lemon cake.... I flip through the pages, past all the meals and treats she made or thought about making, until I get to a page that's not a recipe at all. Or her handwriting. I recognize Dad's distinct, slanted cursive.

He's written lists. Rows upon rows of items, each with a different header. *Food. Utensils. Clothing. Tools. Medicine. Weapons.*

My mind scrambles to make sense of what I'm looking at. When did Dad write these? And why in Mom's recipe book?

I glance toward the door to make sure he's not about to walk in and flip to another page, expecting to see more lists. Instead there's some sort of rectangular diagram, like a blueprint, neatly sketched and labeled in pencil. It looks like a room or very small apartment, complete with a couch, a tiny kitchen, two bunk beds, and a little squared-off space for a bathroom. I squint at the cramped printing. *Food/supplies, storage, shelving, stairs, entrance*—each word accompanied by a little arrow pointing to its designated spot in this...what is this?

Outside the rectangle are the words *Air filtration system.* But why would this room need an air filtration system?

Then it hits me. It's because it would be underground.

My father has drawn up plans for an underground bunker.

Chapter Two

I stay up until after midnight finishing Claire's bracelet. Focusing on the intricate knotting pattern is the only thing I can do to keep my mind off of the recipe book.

Until I go to bed, where there's nothing to do but think. My body feels tired, but my brain is wide awake with images of canned goods and respirator masks and tactical knives. All the things on my father's lists. Sweat gathers on my skin, and I kick off the blanket. He's cataloged exactly what we would need to survive a real apocalypse.

I finally drift off around two a.m., lulled by the patter of rain on my window. The next morning, it's pouring and my limbs are heavy with exhaustion. Claire's car appears in the gloom and I sprint, trying not to get soaked as I throw myself into her messy landfill of a front seat. I shake out my hair, dripping water all over her dashboard. Oops.

"So, I'm freaking out," she says as we pull away. Our rides to school are routine at this point, and she's not one to bother with small talk. "Ms. Grandy posted the grades for that precalc unit test we had last week. You know, the one I thought went pretty well?"

I lift my head and try to look alert. "And did it?"

"No." Claire flicks the wipers to the highest speed. "I got a seventy-six, Iz. A *seventy-six*. It brought my grade down like five points. And we have the final exam coming up, which is worth *thirty* per cent."

"You'll do fine," I say calmly. The tightness in my stomach releases a little. Listening to my best friend spiral over school feels normal and familiar, and comforting her is making me feel better, too. "It's next year that really matters anyway. Colleges don't care about your junior year grades unless you're applying early. So it's not worth worrying about."

She glances at me, eyes wide. "I *am* applying early. Aren't you?"

"I mean, yeah. Probably. But art school focuses more on the portfolio. I don't really need to worry about precalc." I shrug.

Sometimes I wonder how Claire and I ever got to be friends. She takes advanced sciences and math and gym; I take art and design and the bare minimum of everything else. She wants to go to a good college and study civil engineering; I'm not even entirely sure what that is. I want to go to art school and study jewelry design and metalsmithing. She's athletic and slim with thick auburn hair; I inherited my mom's wide hips and incoordination and my dad's dull brown hair and slightly-too-big nose. If the proximity of our lockers hadn't thrown us together daily in ninth grade, we probably never would have gotten close.

"You amaze me, Isobel," Claire says with a shake of her head. "How do you do it? How do you *not* worry about the future?"

"Because the future is unpredictable," I reply. "Things change. Plans go awry. Forty-one-year-old moms die of cancer. The way I see it, worrying about what may or may not happen is pointless."

Claire nods. "Good point."

She parks the car as close as possible to the school, but we're still dripping by the time we get inside. Her first class is right across from my locker, so we head there.

"Are you okay?" Claire asks as we shoulder our way through the hallway crowd.

"Yeah, why?"

"Because your concealer isn't enough to hide those dark circles and you didn't even notice Miguel walking by."

I blink and glance behind me, but Miguel—Claire's friend and the focus of a tiny unrequited crush I've been harboring for weeks—has been absorbed into the crowd. "Oh, I almost forgot," I say, sidestepping her concern. "I have something for you."

I wait until we're at my locker, then I unhook my backpack from my shoulder and unzip the front pocket. Inside, wrapped in several pieces of tissue paper, is the ladder wrap bracelet.

Claire's face lights up. "Oh my God, it's gorgeous. Thank you." She carefully slips the bracelet onto her narrow wrist. "You're so talented, Iz."

I smile. "Just try not to lose it on the soccer field."

The bell rings, and I have only three minutes to get to English on the opposite side of the school. I fling open my locker to stow my jacket and gather my things, an action that's usually automatic for me. But today, I just stand there, frozen and staring.

The long rectangular shape seems to contort into neat lines and sharp corners, carefully drawn in pencil. Suddenly, I'm overcome by a strange suffocating feeling as I stare into the small space. My dented locker fades away, and I see a room—four walls, a low concrete ceiling, metal bed frames, a tiny kitchen. *A bunker.*

My lungs constrict as if I'm in that room right now, the air getting thinner until there's barely enough left to draw a breath. The damp earth surrounds me, pressing me deeper underground, so strong I'll never break free from the weight of it. *Trapped.*

Last fall, Dad "gifted" April and me with bug-out bags. Maybe I should've known then that my father had turned a corner in his quest for preparedness. For months, half my closet has been taken up by an extra-large tan backpack, its sides bulging with enough emergency survival supplies to keep me going for seventy-two hours after disaster strikes. Until now, I've mostly ignored its hulking presence in my room, hiding it when Claire comes over because I don't want her to know how excessive my dad can be. But after yesterday, I can't help wondering how far he'll go to protect us from some hypothetical apocalypse.

As far as drawing up plans for a bunker, apparently.

Would he actually build that thing? In our backyard? And what does he think is going to happen to us that we'd need a hidden, underground fortress?

"Iz? You okay?"

I look over at Claire, shoving the strange feeling down as fast as it came up. I could talk to her about Dad—she was there for me two years ago during the horrible months Mom was sick, and the even more horrible months after she died—but how would I even explain it to her? I don't want people to think of my father as some weirdo in a tinfoil hat.

"I'm fine," I say. When I look at my locker again, it's back to being just a dented old locker.

Chapter Three

I'm packing up my supplies after art class when Ms. Sheridan appears beside me. "Isobel," she says with her usual lively enthusiasm. My art teacher radiates pep, the kind that comes from way too much caffeine. "Your final project is coming along great."

I smile. "Thanks."

The theme of our final project is mixed media art. Mine is a silhouette of a bird, cut from a piece of newspaper and surrounded by color-pencil sketches of feathers and old-fashioned cages. I still need to add in a tree branch for its perch—which I'll do in acrylic paint—but so far I'm pleased with how it's shaping up.

"Very creative." Ms. Sheridan slides her glasses to the top of her head and leans forward, squinting down at my project. She traces the outline of the bird with her ink-splotched finger. "I love the disparity you're showing here—the bird front and center, her mouth open in song, obviously free yet surrounded by all these restrictive cages."

"Thanks," I repeat, zipping my backpack. She's big on assigning meaning to whatever art we make, even if it sucks. But I have to admit, that's exactly what I was going for.

"Possible contender for your portfolio, do you think?"

I examine what I have so far, trying to see it objectively. "Maybe, if it turns out."

She smiles and crosses her fingers. Ms. Sheridan has been really supportive since I told her I'm planning on applying to art school next year. She went to Chapman College of Art and Design after she graduated from teachers' college, and she thinks it could be a possibility for me.

Sure, it's a possibility...just like most dreams. Chapman is considered one of the best art schools in the country and it's notoriously hard to get into, not to mention about fifteen hundred miles from here. Still, it's the only art school that offers a major in jewelry and metalworking.

Going there would mean leaving Dad and April, which is even harder to imagine now with...everything. I'll probably end up going to a local art school and living at home.

If home is still home by then, I remind myself, *and not a bunker underground.*

Ms. Sheridan pops her glasses back on and looks at me. "You know, Isobel, it's not often I get a student with your range of talent and potential. I think you have a really good shot at Chapman." She winks behind her thick lenses. "Especially if an alumna puts in a good word for you."

A really good shot. A warm buzzy feeling fills my body. Maybe this dream isn't so farfetched.

Claire left school early for a dentist appointment, so I take the bus home in the rain. My brain is still humming from what Ms. Sheridan said, so I barely notice my phone vibrating in the front pocket of my backpack. It's probably just Dad, checking in to make sure I got home from school okay like he does every day.

By the time I get dropped off at the end of my street, it's pouring. The wind has picked up, and flashes of lightning streak through the slate-gray sky. As I sprint toward my house, the air smells of wet pavement and electricity. Thunder rumbles in the distance, and I slow my pace for a moment and tip my face to the darkening sky. Lightning flashes again, followed by a clap of thunder so loud I feel it in my chest. There's something empowering about being outside during a storm.

Inside the entryway, I step out of my wet shoes and unzip my jacket, trying not to drip all over the tile. The house is dim and stuffy, and for a second it seems like no one's home. Then I hear the TV—some guy talking about air masses. The Weather Network, by the sounds of it. I bend over to peel off my damp socks.

"Where have you been?"

I look up, and my father is standing at the threshold to the living room, his hair ruffled like he just ran his fingers through it. I straighten, forgetting about my other sock. "I was talking to my art teacher after school. Guess what? She said—"

"Why didn't you text me you were going to be late?"

I take off my other sock and frown at him. Why is he freaking out? "I didn't even know you were home until I saw the car in the driveway," I say. "It was important, Dad. Ms. Sheridan wanted to talk to me about art school."

He stares at me with a hollow expression, then shakes his head and disappears into the living room. Confused, I follow him, dripping rainwater on the laminate floor. He stops in front of the coffee table and grabs the remote, pointing it at the TV. The volume rises.

"I texted you," my father says, his eyes on the screen and his back to me. A reporter dressed in rain gear is stationed on the waterfront area downtown, yelling into her microphone about localized flooding. "Why didn't you answer me?"

I look at my backpack, still sitting on the ceramic tile where I left it. "I didn't hear my phone, I guess." Lying is easier than admitting I ignored his text because I was daydreaming and didn't want one of his check-ins to yank me back to reality. "Why? What's going on?"

"A funnel cloud touched down about five hundred miles from here," he says, his voice an octave higher than usual. "There's a chance a tornado watch could be issued for us too." He gestures toward the TV. "A *tornado* on the east coast. These storms are getting worse. I hate that we live so close to the ocean."

My mind spins back to the hurricane we had the fall after Mom died. The warnings on TV. The subtle shift in the air as the wind grew and the sky darkened. The anxious gleam in Dad's eyes as he boarded up our windows, a thin barrier against the force of Mother Nature.

I glance around the room. No blocked windows this time, but the curtains are shut tight, a thick fabric barricade against the bright flashes outside. Dad's expression is the same, though—like he's bracing himself for whatever's coming. It douses my excitement, though it's still there, bubbling, pushing through the weird tension in the room.

"Dad, I wanted to talk to you about my plans for next year," I press. Maybe I can distract him, get him interested in the future. *My* future. "Ms. Sheridan says I have a good chance of getting into Chapman. You know, that art school near Traci and Heath?" Traci and Heath are my godparents. Traci was my mom's best friend—they met in nursing school and stayed close even after Traci moved away, right up until Mom's death. She still calls to check in on us a few times a month.

"Chapman is only a forty-five-minute drive from their house," I continue, "so maybe they'd be cool with me living with them if I get accepted. I wasn't even going to apply, but Ms. Sheridan went there and might be able to pull some strings, and if my portfolio is strong enough, maybe...." I pause when I realize he's barely listening. "Dad?"

He doesn't even look at me. "We'll talk about it later." He walks over to the window, shifting the curtain aside to peer into the bleak wet gray. "You shouldn't have been outside, Isobel."

"Dad," I say again, this time with force. It scares me when he gets in his head like this. "Look at me. I'm fine. I didn't get hit by lightning or sucked up into a tornado." *That's not even anywhere near us*, I think. "I just got wet."

He tears his gaze away from the window, taking in my dripping hair and soaked jeans. The lines around his eyes relax a bit, and he comes over to me, placing a rough hand on my damp head. I lean into it, inhaling his customary scent of Irish Spring soap and fresh lumber. "Next time, answer my texts," he says softly. "Okay?"

"Okay," I say, just to get us off the topic. "Why are you home early, anyway?"

"April had a stomachache, so I picked her up from school." He sits on the chair, which is closest to the TV, and places the remote on the arm. "I gave her some ginger ale, and now she's taking a nap."

I nod, somewhat relieved. I half thought he'd gotten a storm warning on his phone and rushed home in the middle of work. All we need is for him to get himself fired.

I leave Dad to his weather updates and head down the hall to check on April. Her door is open a crack. I peek inside to see her sitting up on her bed, brushing her Barbie doll's long, black hair and humming a song from *Frozen*. A crash of thunder shakes the house, but she barely even flinches.

"Feeling better?"

"A little," she says. Then her eyes widen as she notices the state I'm in. "Did you go outside?"

"Yeah."

Her eyes grow even wider. "In the tornado?"

Oh man. Either Dad told her about the funnel cloud, or she overheard us talking in the living room. Probably the latter.

"There's no tornado," I assure her. "And even if there was a tornado, we'd be okay."

She nods and sections off the doll's hair for a braid, the way I taught her. "Because Daddy would protect us."

"Right," I say, because that's how most kids think of their dads.

"Izzie?" She stops braiding and looks at me. "Was Mommy scared of storms and stuff, like Daddy is?"

"Not really. She was more like you and me."

April smiles, pleased, and goes back to braiding her Barbie doll's hair. I head for the bathroom. I need to get out of these wet clothes and into a warm shower.

The bathroom is as dark as the living room, the single window shielded by closed blinds. Only here, alone, do I grab the attached strings and pull, filling the room with muted light.

Chapter Four

"Hey, girls." Dad pauses at the threshold to the living room, where April and I are stretched out on the rug making friendship bracelets. "I need to run into the city for a bit. Back in a couple of hours."

"But Dad…" I say as he turns away. "I have homework. I can't watch April all afternoon."

He pauses, frowning. "Oh. Well, this is kind of important, so—"

April jumps up. "I want to go with you, Daddy."

"Oh," Dad says again, this time hesitantly. "I don't think so, Sunshine. You'd probably get bored."

I put down my embroidery floss and peer up at him. What's with the secrecy?

"Please?" April dances around, arms flailing like one of those inflatable tube people in front of car dealerships. "I'm bored *now*."

I frown at her barely started bracelet. Unlike me, April likes to be in constant motion, dancing and making messes and running around outside. But it's been raining nonstop for six days, and Rana's off somewhere with her family, so she's been stuck inside with me and my desperate attempts to keep her entertained.

Dad smiles, relenting. "Well, I suppose it'll be okay. There might be other kids there too."

"Other kids *where*?" I ask.

His eyes take on that increasingly familiar gleam. "Weldon Preparedness Group is having their meeting at the library downtown. I missed the last one, so I'd really like to catch this month's."

April jumps up and down, excited at the prospect of a library trip.

"Weldon Preparedness Group?" I ask over her squeals.

"People get together and discuss how to prepare for disaster situations." He goes to the hallway closet and takes out April's raincoat. "A lot of places have groups like this now. I found them online."

A disturbing image pops into my head of my little sister surrounded by a bunch of gloomy people discussing things like catastrophic storms and tsunamis.

Nope. Not on my watch.

I don't have the heart to make April stay at home with me and my crafts, so I grab my raincoat too. Homework can wait until later. At least at the library, I can distract her with books.

The library is packed. Dad grabs April's hand as the three of us head for the stairs. Weldon Public Library is massive, with three floors and several meeting rooms. Dad leads us up to the top, where there's a wall of windows overlooking the city. April catches sight of the colorful children's section in the corner and lunges toward it, but Dad pulls her back.

"Hang on a sec, Sunshine. I want to introduce you guys to some people first."

Oh God. The last thing I want to do is have a meet-and-greet with a roomful of doomsday preppers. But I have to stick close to April, so I don't object when my father ushers us into one of the meeting rooms.

At first, I assume we're in the wrong room. When Dad mentioned the preparedness group, I pictured dozens of people, mostly guys my dad's age who look slightly mountain-man-esque like he does, with his beard and ponytail and tattoos. But there are only ten adults here, some mingling and others sitting on folding chairs that have been arranged in a circle around the middle of the room. Out of all of them, Dad's the only one who looks like he could be cast on a doomsday prepper reality show.

When did he join this group? It's like he has a whole other life that I know nothing about.

April and I get introduced around. We meet Gail and Stuart, a white-haired elderly couple. Charlene and Kiana, two middle-aged hippy-ish women. Nick, a pale, thirtysomething red-haired guy. Kendra and James, a young Black couple, and their baby boy Micah. Jun, a grandmotherly-looking Asian woman. And Dennis and Roberta, a white couple who appear to be in their fifties. They're all vastly different, yet ordinary, the kind of people you'd expect to see in the library on a Saturday afternoon.

"You have beautiful daughters, Gabe," Gail, the white-haired lady, tells my father. She looks at April as she says it, so I'm not sure why she pluralized *daughter*. "I hope you bring them to meetings more often."

Dad just smiles serenely while I stand there awkwardly and April twirls around my legs. Luckily, the fifty-something guy—Dennis—chooses this moment to step forward and clap a few times, commanding everyone's attention.

"Okay, folks, let's get started."

I'm not surprised that he's the leader of the group. He's tall and imposing, with ramrod-straight posture and a neat buzz cut. His vibe screams ex-military. Everyone in the room, including his tiny wife, looks at him with a hint of awe. It's creepy.

"It's good to see you all," Dennis goes on, smiling as the rest of the group—minus April and me—takes a seat. "Now, today will be a fairly standard meeting, but I urge you to stick around until the end because Roberta and I have some big news to share." He winks at his wife, who beams up at him. "Okay, first order of business. Has anyone learned anything new that might be useful to the group?"

The redhead—Nick—raises a hand. "As you guys know, I've been working on building a Faraday cage. At first I was using a standard bird cage, but the holes were too big. So I ended up building a wooden frame and attaching aluminum screen mesh to it. I'm really pleased with how it turned out."

Dennis nods at him. "Excellent, Nick. Solar flares and electromagnetic pulses are a legitimate threat to civilization. We should all have a protected space for our important data and electronics."

April tugs on my hand. When I look down, she whispers, "What's a solar flare?"

I take this as my cue to get her the hell out of here. I'm not exactly sure what a solar flare is either, but it's probably not something a small child needs to worry about.

Dad's completely riveted to the Fara-whatever discussion, so it takes a few seconds to get his attention. I signal to him that we're leaving, then take April's hand and slip out as quietly as possible. No one seems to notice.

Stepping out into the bright, airy main section, I feel like I can breathe again. April and I make a beeline for the children's area. She marches directly toward a display shelf and grabs a book with a cartoon horse on the cover. If there's anything my sister loves, it's horses. And unicorns. And elephants. And most other large animals.

"Izzie, can you read this to me?" she asks, already flipping through the pages.

I always melt a little when she calls me Izzie. That was Mom's name for me. "How about *you* read it to *me?*"

We find a vacant chair by the window and settle in. April's short attention span isn't made for quiet activities, but we manage to make it through three books before she gets bored. We visit the bathroom, then gaze out the window for a while until April loses interest and starts zigzagging through the stacks.

"April," I whisper-scold when I finally catch up to her in nonfiction. "You need to stay where I can see you."

She nods and skips to the end of the aisle. I'm torn between watching her and checking out the arts and crafts books in front of me. The books win. I spot a large, full-color book on jewelry-making and slide it off the shelf.

I'm engrossed in a page about wirework techniques when April bolts away again. I shove the book back into its slot and hurry after her. If she escapes down the stairs, who knows where she'll end up. I find her a few aisles away, standing at the opposite end and grinning like we're playing a game. In my haste to reach her, I bump into some guy who's crouched in the middle of the aisle, perusing the bottom shelf.

"Oops, sorry," I say. My gaze is immediately drawn to the tan-colored bracelet on his wrist. Hemp, I think.

"It's okay." He looks up and smiles. His eyes are a deep liquid brown, and I forget about the preparedness people, and April, and everything else.

"Izzie." Sweaty little fingers curl around my hand, snapping me out of my daze. "I want to see Daddy now."

I shift my gaze to April's face, now flushed from running. Mine's probably flushed too, the result of colliding with an attractive boy. "Let's go," I say, taking her hand and leading her away. As I do, I peek at the section he's in. Medicine.

The doomsday gathering is still going when we get back to the room. Someone propped the door open, so no one notices as April and I slip inside and move toward the back of the room. Content now that Dad is in her sight, April sits cross-legged on the carpeted floor and pulls Twilight Sparkle, the purple My Little Pony toy she takes with her everywhere, from her sweatshirt pocket. I yawn and lean against the wall. This meeting has got to be over soon.

"That's a great point, Kendra," Dennis is saying. "An international cyberattack could wipe out the financial industry. We rely too much on technology these days." He glances at his watch, then at his wife, who gives a slight nod and stands up to join him. "Now. As promised, Roberta and I have some big news."

Everyone watches him, waiting. Most of them have their backs to me—including my father—so I can't see their faces. I imagine they're all giving him that deferential gaze.

"We're leaving in three weeks," Dennis announces.

There's a chorus of protests and questions. Dennis just smiles, his eyes sharp as he assesses their reaction.

"You mean for good?" someone asks.

"Where are you going?"

Dennis shifts closer to his wife and wraps his arm around her shoulders. "Roberta and I have joined Endurance Ranch."

"Endurance Ranch," Nick exclaims. "The survival community out near Westlake Forest?"

"That's right," Dennis says. "You've heard of it?"

"Hell yes. That place is equipped to withstand almost anything. Marauder threats, natural disasters, radioactive fallout, you name it. Believe me, it's the place you want to be when the collapse happens."

When? Is this dude psychic? Can he see into the future?

My snarky thoughts are interrupted when someone walks in the room. To my shock, it's the boy I almost plowed down in the stacks. He notices April and me as he passes, and a flicker of surprise crosses his face. Then he looks away again and goes to sit in the empty chair next to the hippy women. One of them—I forget their names—reaches up to brush a wayward lock of hair off his face, a parental gesture. They look alike, with similar olive skin and thick black hair.

"Couldn't agree more, Nick," Dennis continues. "Endurance Ranch is a sixty-acre compound that backs up to a fifteen-thousand-acre forest. Fully sustainable with crops and livestock and a year's worth of stockpiled food and supplies. There's even a medical clinic."

"What about lodging?" the man with the baby asks.

"There are several log homes with basement shelters," Roberta says. "And they're currently building a big underground shelter with over a dozen rooms."

Underground shelter. So it's not just my father who's into the whole bunker idea. I peek over at him. I can't see his face, but he's stroking his beard like he does whenever he's thinking.

"A brand-new shelter means a lot more room," Dennis adds. Then he pauses, his eyes shining in a way that reminds me of Dad's. "Which means the community is currently open to new members."

"How many new members?" the elderly man asks.

"Dozens more. They're looking for people like us, folks who see the world clearly and will do whatever it takes to protect our families." He runs a hand over his buzzed hair. "Survival communities aren't just for the wealthy anymore. The ranch is designed for intelligent, working-class people who are willing to chip in and keep the place running. It's the only place of its kind in the entire country."

"Exactly how far is it from here?" asks the blond hippy woman.

"About two thousand miles. And if you're thinking that's too far away, then you're absolutely right. That's why Roberta and I are moving to Holcomb, the closest town to the ranch. There's no point in joining a survival community if you can't get there quickly when the shit hits the fan."

Everyone nods, like moving halfway across the country to be near a doomsday ranch makes perfect sense. Who *are* these people? I stand up straight, feeling more uneasy by the second.

"The new shelter is going to fill up fast," Dennis goes on. "So if you're interested in securing a spot, you should act soon. Just make sure you know what you're getting into before you make the commitment. This could mean a significant lifestyle change. We're talking about uprooting your entire life here. Dropping everything and moving your family halfway across the country. And once you're in, you're not going to want to give up your spot."

The room goes silent as everyone mulls over Dennis's words. I look down at April. She's playing quietly with her pony, seemingly oblivious to the conversation.

"So," Dennis says after a moment, "how about we see a show of hands? Who here thinks they might be interested in joining Endurance Ranch?"

There's another, longer pause, and then hands slowly start to rise, one by one. My body goes cold when I realize that one of them belongs to my father.

Chapter Five

I don't speak a word to Dad the entire drive home. My jaws ache with the storm of words inside me—but this isn't a confrontation I want April to see. It's not until after dinner, when she's off playing at Rana's house, that I get my chance.

Dad is in the backyard, fixing a loose bolt on the swing set. The rain finally tapered off, but it's still damp and chilly outside, too chilly for the thin T-shirt I'm wearing. The cold is the least of my worries.

My father looks up as I approach, my shoes squelching loudly in the wet grass. He's wearing his black bandanna, and for a moment I can imagine him as he might have been twenty years ago, back when he drove a motorcycle and played drums in a rock band. *He was the bad boy with the heart of gold*, Mom would say whenever I asked about their early dating days. Cringey description aside, I got what she meant. Still, I never understood how two such different people managed to fall in love.

"What's up, Tater?" he asks, focusing on the bolt again.

I cross my arms, annoyed. My middle name is Tate, so when the mood strikes him, he calls me *Tater* or *Tater Tot*. But I don't want to hear it right now.

"Dad," I say, stepping closer. "You can't...you're not actually serious about joining that ranch place. Right?"

His wrench goes still as his gaze snaps up to mine. His surprise tells me he didn't know April and I were there, watching and listening.

"I wish you hadn't heard that," he says, turning back to the swing set. "Nothing is for sure yet."

"Yet?" The word comes out as a squeak. "What does that mean?"

"Isobel, honey—"

"So, what happens if we join this place?" I cut in. "You can't just drag us halfway across the country because you're afraid of...." I shake my head. It doesn't matter. "Our lives are *here*. What would you do, quit your job and pull April and me out of school? You can't expect us to go along with this."

Dad sighs and drops the wrench into his jacket pocket. "I still need to research the place. I'm not making any decisions right now."

"Well, I've made *my* decision. I'm not going, and neither is April."

"Don't forget who the parent is here, Isobel," he says, his tone rising to meet mine. "We'll do whatever I think is best for this family."

"And what's best for this family is ripping us away from our home to live with a bunch of doomsday preppers? I think you've been hanging around that Dennis guy too much." I glance around, grateful that our backyard is surrounded by a tall fence. But the neighbors can probably hear us, so I lower my voice. "You heard what he said. There's no point in joining if you don't live near enough to get there quickly in case the world blows up or whatever."

"I'm not saying we'd move there," Dad says more calmly. "But we could visit the ranch for a couple of weeks or so, see if we like it. Would that be so bad? I'm sure it's a beautiful place. Staying there wouldn't be much different from a vacation."

"Except vacations are fun and you're generally not forced to go against your will," I say wryly. "That Dennis guy said that once you secure your spot at the ranch, you're not going to want to give it up. So why travel all that way if you're not sure you're serious about it?"

"This isn't the type of decision you make lightly, Isobel." Dad shakes the swing set to test it for sturdiness. "Nothing is decided. If we went there and found it wasn't for us, then I'd find ways to protect us here at home."

"How, by building an underground bunker?" The words burst from my mouth, like they'd been waiting at the back of my tongue for days. I expect a flash of surprise, or embarrassment, *something*, but he just stares at me, unblinking. "I saw the sketch in Mom's blue recipe book," I add. "And the lists."

"I did that years ago, right after...." He looks away and shuts his eyes for a moment. *Right after Mom died.* He meets my gaze again, his eyes hard and determined. "But yes. If it comes down to it, I'll build a bunker. Someday we might be glad to have it."

Someday. "So, you're saying I have a choice between some ranch in the middle of nowhere or a bunker underneath my backyard." I laugh at the ridiculousness of it, but my amusement quickly shifts to tears. "No offense, Dad, but I think I'd rather take my chances with the apocalypse."

His expression softens, and he lifts an arm as if to comfort me. I back away, out of his reach.

"Mom would hate the way you're acting," I tell him. I watch his face fall, then turn and go back inside the house.

Whenever I feel like I need my mom the most, I go out to the driveway and sit in her car.

Technically, it's my car now, though I've never driven it. Whenever Dad takes me out to practice driving, it's always in his Ford Explorer. Neither of us has acknowledged it, but I think we both feel like Mom's car is kind of sacred, and that driving it might break the spell. But sitting in the driver's seat is okay. For some reason, it helps.

This time, though, the comfort isn't kicking in. Right after my fight with Dad, I grabbed my sketchbook and headed straight for the silver Elantra. I've been in here for over an hour and I still haven't calmed down.

Maybe it's because my mother's presence has faded. When I first started hanging out in here, right after she died, she was everywhere: Her scent, a mixture of coconut shampoo and the sanitizing gel she rubbed on her hands during her nursing shifts, embedded in the seat fabric. Her collection of gum packages and lip balms in the cubby beneath the stereo. Her name on the insurance papers in the glove box. The purple ribbon charm she'd hung on the rearview mirror right after her pancreatic cancer diagnosis. Her essence surrounded me.

Now, all I can smell is the musty scent of unused car. April made off with the gum and lip balms a while ago, and Dad eventually removed the insurance papers. All that's left is the purple ribbon and the memories I have of her sitting exactly where I am now, her chapped hands on the steering wheel, fingers tapping to the Top 40 songs she liked to listen to on the radio.

The memories, at least, will stay fixed in here forever.

I force myself to focus on a new dangle earring design I've been working on in my sketchbook. Soon, I'm lulled by the scratch of pencil as I bring the images in my head to the paper. I'm so engrossed, in fact, that I almost jump out of my skin when the passenger side door opens and April flings herself inside.

"What are you doing?" she asks, slamming the door closed.

I flick the pad shut and stick my pencil into the coils. "Designing something." I tug one of her curls. "Shouldn't you be getting ready for bed?"

"Just a few more minutes?" she asks hopefully. I'm too tired to argue, and she grins. Her gaze moves up to the purple ribbon charm. "Tell me about Mommy."

This is a little game we play sometimes. I call them Mom Facts. April was only four when Mom died; she remembers her, but mostly in an abstract kind of way. Mom Facts help bring her to life.

I think for a minute, trying to come up with something I haven't already told her. "She *really* loved hotdogs," I say. "She couldn't resist a hotdog piled high with mustard and onions. One time when we went to a carnival, she ate four of them in a row."

April giggles. "Four?"

I laugh with her. These are the types of facts I always choose to share with her—the nice ones. The funny ones. Like how Mom sang—badly—whenever she was washing dishes or folding the laundry. Or how she told us funny stories about her geriatric nursing patients at dinner. Or how, when she was pregnant with me, she was so obsessed with *Grey's Anatomy* that she named me after one of the main characters, and then did the same thing when April was born eleven years later.

These are the only facts my sister needs to know right now. She doesn't need to know about the bad ones. The scary ones. Like how Mom dismissed her fatigue and back pain at first because she was the mother of a small child and all parents with small children are tired and sore. Like how, by the time she realized something was wrong, the cancer had already spread to her liver, lymph nodes, and lungs. How sick and thin she became during the months of chemo and radiation and surgeries, only to have the cancer spread farther and faster until, finally, it reached her brain. And how the last time I saw her alive, she was lying in a hospital bed, bald and unconscious and covered in tubes. Dad had held her hand to his dripping face and whispered apologies, over and over, for not being able to protect her from the monster that had invaded her body and reduced it to skin-covered bones.

No. April deserves to hear only the good things.

"Izzie?"

I clear the lump from my throat. "Yeah?"

April bites her lip, and I brace myself for a difficult question, like that time she asked Dad if he was going to die too, like Mommy. But all she says is, "Do you think Daddy will let me do horseback riding?"

A laugh bubbles out of me. I marvel at how easily she can switch from memories of Mom to everything else. This is why I tell her only the good stuff. "Maybe. Unless you're as allergic to horses as you are to cats and dogs."

"I'm not," she says firmly, like she could make it true with her sheer, six-year-old will. "I'm gonna ask."

She hops out of the car and runs toward the open garage, where our father has appeared. I watch through the windshield as April skids to a stop in front of him, her mouth already moving. He smiles down at her as she talks, her hands gesturing wildly like Mom's used to do whenever she told a story. When she's finished, he says something before placing a hand on her head and pointing her toward the house. She skips away happily, so clearly he didn't tell her no.

My gaze shifts back to Dad, who's now peering through the dimness in my direction. When he spots me, sitting motionless in the driver's seat of Mom's car, his eyes widen for a moment, like he's looking at a ghost. Then he blinks and turns away, like he never noticed me there at all.

Chapter Six

A few nights later, I'm taking out the trash when I hear a voice coming from the front of the house. Two voices—Dad's and someone else's. At first, I think he's talking to one of the neighbors, but when I move closer, I see an unfamiliar truck parked along the curb. I pause at the corner of the house, beside the garage. The second voice is vaguely familiar.

"Most of the management is former military, like me. That's why they were so eager to have us on board. A retired Navy lieutenant commander who served in two wars and a farmer's daughter? The place is made for Roberta and me."

It clicks. The second voice is Dennis, from the Weldon Preparedness Group. The one who introduced my father to the idea of Endurance Ranch.

I move closer to the house and duck into the shadows, where I can eavesdrop without them seeing me.

"It's made for you too, Gabe," Dennis goes on. "You'd be a great asset for the team building the new shelter. They're desperate for members like you. Did I mention the crew gets to live right on the ranch during construction? You wouldn't even have to rent a place nearby."

I hold my breath, waiting for Dad's answer. But all I hear is the thump of the garage fridge closing, followed by the *click-fizz* of cans being opened.

"It's a big decision," Dad finally responds.

"Sure." Dennis pauses. "A big decision, but not a hard one. At least not for Roberta and me. I mean, look at the sorry state of the world right now. You saw what happened with Hurricane Katrina: the chaos, all those displaced people. You think that won't keep happening? We need to take control of our situation instead of sitting around waiting for civilization to crumble any more than it already has."

My jaws tighten. I have to hand it to the guy—he knows exactly how to appeal to my father. I'm not sure if every doomsday prepper is like him, but Dad's thing has always been natural disasters.

"Yeah," Dad says. "We do need to take control."

There's a shuffling of feet. I pull back, flattening myself against the siding.

"Russell Pruitt is the man to contact about membership for you and your girls," Dennis says, his voice a bit closer now. "He runs the ranch. Retired Air Force colonel. Here's his email and phone number. Tell him I sent you."

"I appreciate it, Dennis. And thanks for stopping in to say good-bye."

"Of course." More shuffling. "I suppose it's not really a good-bye, though."

The unspoken question hangs in the cool night air. I keep perfectly still, trying to ignore the hammering heartbeat in my ears.

"Well, then," my father says. "I guess we should say 'see you soon.'"

I turn and slink back to the yard, my hands numb on the fence gate as I lock it quietly behind me.

I'm waiting at the kitchen table when Dad emerges from April's room a half hour later. My stomach feels like it's harboring its own storm, forceful and churning.

"Oh," Dad says when he walks in to find me here, sitting with my fingers curled around Mom's vintage saltshaker duck. "I thought you were in your room."

I slide the duck back into place, next to its twin peppershaker. "April asleep?"

"Out like a light."

He fills a glass with water and sips it like everything is normal. The storm in my gut intensifies.

"Dennis was here." There's no point in pretending I hadn't seen him.

Dad leans against the counter, his expression neutral. "Yes. He came to say good-bye. He and his wife are moving in a few days."

"To Endurance Ranch," I finish for him.

An uneasy silence fills the room. I fiddle with the beaded stretch bracelet on my wrist while Dad drinks his water and avoids my gaze. I don't even need to admit to eavesdropping—he can tell I've reached my own conclusions. When influential leader–types like Dennis get on board with something, they want everyone else to follow. They don't just "drop in to say good-bye" if they see an opportunity to give that one final push. Especially when the person is already so close to the edge.

"Isobel," Dad begins, then pauses to let out a sigh. "I know how you feel about the ranch."

"But..." I prompt when he doesn't continue.

"*But*, I think we need to go."

Even though I knew this was coming, that he'd already made up his mind and it didn't matter what *I* wanted, his words still land hard. "When?" I ask, my voice hollow. "For how long?"

"We'll drive there as soon as school is out. We can stay on the ranch for two weeks to get a feel for the place before buying in. Then, if we like it after that, we'll consider joining." He takes another drink. "Dennis mentioned that they need people with experience in construction to help build the new shelter, so I'm hoping I can be useful while we're there."

"If we do become members, what does that mean, exactly?" I don't want to say what I'm really afraid of. *Do members have to stay there for good?*

"I haven't thought that far ahead yet."

"Well, what about your job?" I ask, trying a new tack. "Are they going to let you take off for that long?"

"I have a few weeks of vacation saved up. It's not a problem." He places his glass on the counter. "Nothing is decided. We'll just have to wait and see."

I start playing with my bracelet again, twisting it until the elastic digs into my skin. "Wait and see," I repeat. I don't buy that. Dad always plans ten steps ahead. "What does *wait and see* mean? We'll see what the doomsday clock looks like at that point? We'll see if we fall in love with the ranch and want to move?"

I feel sick just imagining it. Leaving this house. Leaving our friends. Missing my senior year at Oakfield High. Missing my life. And for what? Some slight possibility that we'll need long-term accommodations for the end of the world?

"Let's just take it one step at a time, okay?"

"I don't want to go," I say, even though I know my choices are limited. I'm under eighteen. A child. We have no extended family, aside from my godmother Traci, but she has no legal claim to me. We'll be off school, so maybe I could convince Dad to let me stay here. No, that wouldn't work either. Even if I did somehow figure a way out of it, Dad would take April. And I can't be separated from her. I don't want to be separated from my father either. Despite everything, he's still my dad, and the only parent I have left.

"I know this is hard for you to understand." Dad pulls out the chair across from me and sits down. "You're like your mom, Isobel. She was perfectly happy to keep her head in the sand. She didn't see the big picture. Didn't understand why I stockpiled food and batteries. Didn't worry about contingencies—she just assumed the world would always be here. She assumed *she'd* always be here, too. She had no will, nothing written down, nothing prepared in case...." His voice trails off, and he looks away, scratching his beard. "She should have been prepared. We all need to be prepared."

My throat tightens. I don't want to prepare to face death when I've barely even lived yet.

"I won't make the same mistake," Dad says, turning back to me. "We need to be ready for what's coming, and Endurance Ranch is our best shot. We're just going to check it out."

The ache of grief in my throat is quickly replaced by stinging anger. He can't seriously be equating Mom's death to the collapse of society. Losing her *felt* like the end of the world, but it wasn't. It was the end of a lot of things, but not everything. The world kept spinning and we kept moving. Or at least April and I did.

"I don't *care* about what's coming, Dad," I bite out, my voice shaky with frustration. "I care about what's already here. I care about *now*."

His mouth opens like he's going to say something, but I don't stick around to hear it. I go to my room and slam the door, not even caring if it wakes April. My father can deal with it.

Chapter Seven

Claire shoves aside a pile of books and loose papers and opens her closet door. "I know it's in here somewhere," she says, rummaging through a row of shirts and jackets, all haphazardly clinging to plastic hangers. Several more lay heaped on the floor of her closet, a small sampling of the chaos that is the rest of her bedroom.

"Claire, it's fine." I try to straighten her quilt, which is a challenge due to her black cat, Marley, who insists on planting herself directly in the middle of the bed. "I don't need any more clothes."

Claire backs out of the closet holding a white off-the-shoulder top. "Found it," she says, then frowns as she watches me tuck in her bedsheets. "What's wrong?"

I flop down next to Marley, who glares at me with her ears back. "Nothing."

"Are you sure? You're tidying, and you usually only tidy my room when something is bothering you. Besides the mess, I mean."

"I'm fine," I say, because avoidance has been my coping strategy of choice since I woke up this morning. My father had already left for work by the time I emerged from my room, so he didn't see me carrying my overnight bag and backpack when I left the house. After school I went straight to Claire's without telling him, which definitely won't go over well, but I need some distance. I also want to prove to him that everything will be okay even when I don't adhere to all his rules and plans.

"Okay." Thankfully, Claire doesn't push. Instead, she shoves the white top at me. "Here, try this on."

I run my fingers over the light, flowy fabric, surprised. Claire is more of a plain T-shirt type. "I've never seen you in this."

"Because I've never worn it. That's why I'm giving it to you." She sits next to me and scratches the cat's head. Marley immediately starts purring, a deep rumble that vibrates the entire bed. "My mother brought it home from one of her business trips. She knows my tastes *so* well."

We laugh, even though I know having checked-out parents bugs her more than she lets on. Maybe avoidance runs deep in the both of us.

I change into the white top, which fits me perfectly.

"Cute," Claire says. "Still a bit chilly to wear it now, but it'll be perfect for one of our cottage parties this summer."

Summer. Every time I think about it, or when someone mentions it, I get this gnawing feeling in my abdomen. There are so many things I want to do—look for a job, practice for my driver's license, work on my portfolio, spend time with Claire at her family's cottage on the beach. But Endurance Ranch threatens all of it.

"If I'm even around," I mutter.

Claire tilts her head at me. "What?"

"Nothing," I say, trying to backpedal. "I mean—we might be going on vacation this summer. Dad and April and me."

Is this what I've been reduced to? Lying to my best friend because I don't know how to explain that my father wants to take us to a survival community? A part of me is afraid that once I admit it to Claire, it'll be real. I'll have no choice but to face it.

"Oh," Claire says, slightly confused. A vacation is something I'd normally tell her about right away. "Where are you going?"

"To visit Traci and Heath." The lie rolls off my tongue, probably because I wish so much that it was true. "Maybe. It's not for sure yet. It's just...a possibility."

Claire nods, her green eyes scanning my face. "That's cool. You don't seem very excited about it, though."

I shrug and exchange the light white top for my own. "Let's watch a movie or something."

We grab chips and chocolate M&M's from the kitchen and bring them to the cozy TV room in the basement. Claire fires up the giant-screen TV, and we decide on a blockbuster sci-fi movie neither of us has seen. As I sink back into the plush sectional couch, relaxing for the first time all night, my phone dings with a text. Then another. A minute later, it starts ringing. I quickly decline Dad's call and mute my notifications. I'm not in the mood for a check-in right now.

Suddenly I'm jolted by a loud explosion, and I refocus my attention on the screen. The scene shifts to a dark, eerie image of the Earth as seen from space, followed by a second explosion as something—an asteroid, I assume—hits the planet with a burst of fire, tearing a hole through the surface. A section of the Earth crumbles like a chunk of dry clay, millions of years of existence destroyed in seconds.

That's all it takes, my father said once when he was going on about a mega-tsunami that wiped out a large portion of Thailand. *Seconds, minutes, and everything's gone.*

But this is just a movie, I remind myself. The Earth will remain reassuringly intact. And we're nowhere near Thailand. We don't get earthquakes and tsunamis here. We're fine.

My self-pep talk doesn't help. The now-familiar dizziness floods over me again, the trapped feeling intensified by the room's darkness. Suddenly, my brain is telling me to get out of here. Fast.

I jump up, startling Claire next to me. "Bathroom," I say before sprinting out of the room.

In the hallway, I bypass the bathroom and head straight for the back door. It's a beautiful evening, balmy and still. I lean my back against the house and take gulps of fresh, warm air, trying to erase the image of the world in flames.

The trapped feeling slowly shifts, and my eyes fill with angry tears. I'm angry at myself for reacting this way. I'm angry at my mother for leaving me to deal with my father on my own. I'm angry at my father for making me overly aware of how vulnerable we are and how quickly our lives can change forever.

"Isobel?" Claire's head pops out the door, her face a mask of concern and confusion. "What happened? What's wrong?"

The sight of my best friend releases something in me. The last few shreds of denial melt away, and my tears turn into sobs.

Claire immediately steps outside and wraps her arm around my shoulders. Neither of us speaks as my sobs gradually recede into gunky sniffles.

"Talk to me, Iz," Claire urges, handing me a crumpled up tissue from her hoodie pocket.

I fold the tissue and wipe my eyes, trying to figure out how—and where—to start. Finally, I settle on, "I'm not going on vacation to visit Traci this summer."

She drops her arm from my shoulders and faces me. "Why not?"

"I lied." My body sags against the house as the hopelessness of the situation hits me. "Dad's actually taking April and me to visit a survival community after school's over."

"He's...a *what*? You're gonna have to catch me up here."

So I do. I tell her everything—Dad's gradual descent into prepper madness, the bunker blueprint, the Weldon Preparedness Group meeting, Dennis, Endurance Ranch. By the time I'm finished, Claire's eyes are two giant orbs.

"Jesus," she says, reaching out to clutch my hand. "Why didn't you tell me this before?"

I dab my nose with the tissue and shrug. "I guess I never thought it'd get this bad, or he'd change his mind about the ranch. And I was embarrassed, I guess. Like, whose father acts like this? I'm so scared he's going to love the place and force us to move there."

"He can't *force* you to go. Can he? I mean, don't you have rights?"

"I'm not an adult yet," I say wearily. "So technically it's up to him."

She sighs and gazes out into the yard and the trees beyond. "What if you stayed here instead? I'll be at soccer camp for two weeks, so you could just sleep in my room. My parents would probably be okay with it. They're never home, anyway."

I shake my head. If only it were as simple as that. "Dad would still take April, and I don't want her going to that place without me." Fresh tears pool in my eyes. "They're the only family I have."

"You have me too, Iz. I'm here for whatever you need."

I swallow. "I really wish that was enough."

Claire squeezes my hand and lets me cry again, which is the best thing she can give me at the moment. When I finally pull myself together, I feel light and calm. Like everything is going to be okay. All the worry and anger has faded to a faint echo.

We stay outside for a while, lounging in a couple of zero-gravity chairs on the deck and talking about random, non-doomsday-related things. It's getting colder as the sun sets, but I don't want to go back inside. I'm content right here, with my best friend beside me and the darkening sky above. Here, right now, the world feels huge and wide open.

Chapter Eight

I'm dreaming about pancakes.

No, not pancakes. Waffles. My eyes pop open, and I sniff the air, the scents of sugar and butter seeping under my bedroom door and filtering through the sleep-fog in my brain. I'm definitely awake now.

When I emerge from the bathroom a few minutes later, I find Dad and April surrounded by a mess in the kitchen. Dad's mixing batter at the counter, while April piles fresh-made waffles onto a platter. The window over the sink is open wide, letting in the warm June breeze. My heart lightens for the first time in days.

"We're making waffles," April announces. She's still in her pajamas, her hair wild and tangled around her face.

"I see that."

Dad tosses me a quick good-morning smile as he pours more batter into the waffle maker. He's freshly showered, his damp brown hair tied back neatly and his beard trimmed short. It hits me then how much better he looks now compared to a few weeks ago. Ever since that library meeting, his face hasn't been as drawn and distracted. His dark circles have almost disappeared. He even looks like he put on some weight. All because of some survivalist community in the woods.

If only I drew as much comfort from the idea.

As the last waffles finish cooking, I grab plates and juice and syrup and set everything on the table. April comes up behind me with forks, and then Dad with the still-steaming waffles. Before he sits down, he lays a hand on my shoulder and squeezes, a silent gesture of truce. I've barely spoken to him since Thursday night, but he's willing to put everything aside for now, if I am.

In response, I briefly meet his eyes as he passes the syrup. *I am.*

The next several minutes are a flurry of talking, laughing, and eating. It feels almost like old times, when Mom was still here, amusing us with work stories. Now it's April who entertains us, only all her stories involve her friend Rana's pet hamster or funny things that happened at school. Going by the soft, wistful way Dad watches her, he's clearly thinking about old times too.

"What should we do today, girls?" Dad asks once breakfast is over. "Go shopping? Go on a hike?"

April wiggles in her chair. "I want to see the horses."

I smile. There's a farm about a fifteen-minute drive away where you can pet the animals and go on pony rides. April went there for a birthday party last fall and she's been obsessed ever since.

"Horses it is. You up for it, Tater?" he asks me, his tone light and cheerful. He's trying his best to smooth over the tension from the weekend. As expected, neglecting to tell him my plans and then ignoring his texts and calls didn't go over well. When I got home from Claire's yesterday, he told me if I didn't start answering my phone when I was out, then I'd be grounded from going out at all.

"I have to study," I say, glad for an excuse. Farm animals and mud aren't really my jam. "Exams start tomorrow."

"Can I ride the pony, Daddy?" April begs, unbothered by my lack of interest.

"Maybe. If the line isn't too long."

She pouts. "I can't wait to go to the ranch. Then I can ride horses every day."

Just like that, the lighthearted vibe is sucked out of the room. I glance sharply at my father, who busies himself clearing the table. He must have told April about the ranch at some point over the weekend, while I was at Claire's. I was worried about how she'd take it, leaving her friends and our home for three weeks, but she seems fine with the idea. Dad clearly used the promise of horseback riding to convince her it was the place to be this summer.

"Okay, Sunshine, go on and get dressed."

April jumps up and bounces out of the kitchen like a human tennis ball. I watch her go before getting up to help my father.

"She's really excited," he says offhandedly as he rinses the plates.

I'm not sure if he's talking about today and the pony rides or this summer and the ranch. "She's excited because she's too young to understand the purpose of the place."

"And I'm thankful for it." He laughs a little. "I'd rather she think about horses than global food shortages and economic collapse."

That's one thing we agree on. I bite back my comments. Dad continues to rinse the dishes, fitting each piece into the dishwasher with careful precision while I scrub away the stickiness from the countertops. Now that we've kind of made up, at least for today, I figure it's a good time to bring up the plan I'd crafted before falling asleep last night.

My hand trembles on the sponge as I try to figure out a way to present it that won't get me shut down immediately.

"Dad," I say gently, "what if April and I stayed with Traci and Heath while you're at the ranch? They're only a few hours away from the place. You could drop us off on the way there and pick us up on your way back."

He shuts the dishwasher and turns to me, frowning. "The whole reason we're going is to see if the ranch works for us as a family. We need to do this together."

"But—"

"Besides," he goes on, "Traci and Heath are way out of the way, in the opposite direction. It would add two extra days to the trip."

I stop scrubbing and toss the dishcloth in the sink. Desperation flares through me, and I scramble for something—anything—to knock him off center. "Have you told Traci about this?"

He avoids my gaze and puts the juice and syrup back in the fridge. "It's not her concern."

"So you haven't told her. Why not?" I don't wait for an answer. "Because you know she wouldn't approve of us driving across the country and being isolated in the woods for weeks? Because she'd tell you this whole idea is *crazy*?"

He shuts the fridge and turns to face me. "Isobel...."

"Well," I say, my eyes steady on his as I draw the last card I have to play, "if you're not going to tell her, I will."

His quiet confidence flickers, but just for a second. "Do whatever you feel you need to, sweetheart," he says, "but it doesn't matter what Traci thinks, because she's not the parent here. I am. We're going to Endurance Ranch."

My hope dissolves with the soap bubbles in the sink. For days, I've been wracking my brain, trying to figure a way out of this. I should have known threats wouldn't work. I should have known he wouldn't want us to stay with Traci, even for a few days. If it were up to him, he'd probably never let us out of his sight again.

After Dad and April leave for the farm, I go to my room and take a stab at studying for my English final. I'm only ten minutes in when my mind starts wandering, the themes in *Julius Caesar* drowned out by echoes of my conversation with Dad this morning. *To see if the ranch works for us as a family.*

What does that mean? Of course it's going to work for him, a doomsday prepper with construction experience. Of course it'll work for April, who loves the outdoors and animals and new adventures. But what about me? What do I have to offer a place like that? I doubt homemade jewelry would be a big hit with the survivalist crowd.

Giving up on *Julius Caesar*, I shove my notes aside and open my laptop. I type *Endurance Ranch* into Google.

I can't keep avoiding facing this just because I don't want it to be true. If this is really happening, like my father said, then I need to be prepared. Just in a different way than he usually means.

The top search result is a website. I click on it, bracing myself for pictures of armed guards and barbed wire. Instead, I'm greeted by the ranch logo—an image of a jaguar head inside a circle—with the words *Prepare, Endure, Thrive* curved beneath it. The rest of the page is mostly text, about the founding of the ranch and what the members hope to achieve. It's nothing I haven't already heard from Dennis and my father.

I click on the *About the Ranch* tab. My screen fills with a list of the ranch's features, followed by a gallery of pictures. I scan through the amenities—underground shelters, riding corrals, stockpiled supplies, quarantine facilities, livestock, and gardens—and zero in on the photos. The first few depict the various basement shelters, apparently located under basic log-cabin-type buildings that look more like vacation cottages than places to hide in the event of Armageddon.

The rest of the pictures remind me of a summer camp brochure, with happy, smiling people engaged in various outdoor activities. Only here, it's mostly adults, and along with canoeing, hiking, and fishing, they're also doing things like hunting and target practice. One picture has a tiny boy holding a child-sized crossbow, aiming his arrow at some unseen target. Is this the kind of thing they do there? Teach children to hunt and defend themselves against "marauders," like Nick from the meeting said to describe potential human threats to the community?

An image of April with a weapon in her hands flickers through my mind. My sweet little sister, who sleeps with a night-light and cries if she accidentally squishes a bug. Despite the sunshine streaming into my room, a chill runs through me.

I haven't given much thought to weapons, though I know the ranch must have a stockpile of those too. Does Dad have any here, in this house? I think about the list he made in Mom's recipe book, the collection of items we'd need to survive an apocalypse. *Weapons* was on there. I shiver again. Mom was strictly anti-gun; she never would have been okay with Dad owning one. But now....

Sometimes I wonder if she'd be disappointed in me for failing to step up in her place. *She* was always able to keep

Dad grounded. *She* would have squashed this ranch idea way before it got this far. But what have I done, besides make threats and complain about the unfairness of it all?

I shut my laptop and lie back on the bed, my chest aching. Most days I'm able to manage living without my mom, but sometimes—like right now—I'd give anything just to feel the warmth of her presence again, assuring me that everything will be okay.

Chapter Nine

I'm in my room, sorting through schoolwork from the year that I no longer need, when I'm interrupted by unfamiliar voices. I stop to listen. It sounds like people talking in our living room. The doorbell rings, followed by more voices. What the hell?

I go to the door and open it a crack. My father passes by the end of the hallway, on his way to the kitchen. Curious, I follow him, glancing into the living room as I pass. Oh God. The redheaded guy. The white-haired couple. The hippy-ish couple. The young couple with the baby. They're all here, save for Dennis and Roberta, who left for Holcomb days ago, and the elderly woman named Jun, who for all I know is headed there too.

The Weldon Preparedness Group. Right here in my living room.

"Isobel," Dad says, surprised to see me standing in the kitchen. "I didn't know you were home."

This isn't surprising, considering we've been avoiding each other all week and only speak when it's absolutely necessary, like when April's around and we want to appear normal for her. Threatening him with Traci either pissed him off, worried him, or a combination of both. In any case, we've been circling each other warily.

I watch as he fills glasses with water and iced tea. "What's going on?" I ask, keeping my voice low. "Why are they here?"

"Oh." He glances toward the living room, his eyes shining brighter than ever. He's definitely found his people, and they aren't us. "I offered to host the monthly meeting. There was some kind of mix-up with the library room we usually have booked, so I invited everyone here instead."

Great. "Where's April?"

"She went to the park with Rana and her parents."

I relax. At least I don't have to worry about her wandering in there and soaking up their end-of-the-world gloom.

"Want to give me a hand with these?" Dad asks, nodding toward the half dozen glasses on the counter.

I don't want to, actually, but I gather up three of the glasses and follow him into the living room. The white-haired lady—the one who told Dad he had beautiful daughters at the library meeting—smiles at me as I place the drinks on the coffee table.

"Are you joining us today, sweetheart?" she asks, her tone sweet and grandmotherly. I try to picture her hunting deer in the woods or pointing a rifle at oncoming marauders.

"Oh, um." I glance around the room, which is noisier and livelier than it's been in years, with people perched on the chairs and sofa, smiling and chatting. As nice as that part may be, I have no interest in sitting through what will probably be an hour-long discussion about Endurance Ranch. "Not today."

At the sound of my voice, everyone stops talking to look at me. Flustered, I turn and go back to the kitchen, even though I don't need anything in there. I consider going to my room, but I'd still hear them through my door, so I pour a glass of iced tea for myself and take it outside to the deck.

The backyard is quiet and still. I sit down in one of the patio chairs and tip my face to the sky, feeling instantly better. From here, the voices inside sound like faint murmurs, far away from my private little spot under the sun.

I left my phone inside, so I'm not sure how much time passes as I sit there, sipping watery iced tea and staring into the trees beyond our fence. The heat of the sun, along with the muffled conversation humming under the soft chirping of birdsong, has lulled me into sort of a trance, so I'm a little startled when I catch a flash of movement out of the corner of my eye. The melting ice in my glass rattles as I stand up and turn toward the open fence gate.

"Sorry. I didn't know anyone was back here."

For a moment, we just stare at each other. Before I stood up, I was expecting to find April at the gate, or maybe a loose dog. What I *wasn't* expecting to find was the dark-haired boy from the meeting at the library, the hippy woman's son.

"What are you doing?" I ask, baffled by his presence in my yard. He looks different in the sunlight, taller and broader, his tan skin flushed with either heat or embarrassment.

"The meeting is here, right?" He gestures toward the house. "I told my parents I'd come by after work. I'm Dane, by the way. Dane Covey."

I glance down at his T-shirt. The words *Jumbo Pretzel* are emblazoned across the front in big red letters. "Isobel," I say, still rattled. "You know, the front door is open."

"Oh. Right. It's just...." He takes a couple of steps forward and points to something at the far end of the yard. "I noticed your patch of chickweed, and I was going to sneak back here and pick some. My mother loves it."

I blink at him, wondering if all that sun has gone to my head. "My patch of what?"

He tucks his fingers into his jeans pockets. "Chickweed. It's an edible plant. Grows in yards and gardens and places like that, though most people try to kill instead of eat it."

"You can eat it?" I look at the area in question, which I always dismissed as a blanket of useless weeds.

"Yeah." He hesitates for a second, then starts walking across the yard. I put down my glass and step off the deck onto the lawn. "The leaves have vitamins," he continues, crouching down and touching one of the tiny white flowers. "You can eat them raw, but they're better when they're cooked. They taste kind of like spinach."

I wrinkle my nose. Spinach isn't my favorite. "How do you know all that?"

He straightens up and brushes off his hands. "My moms are experienced survivalists. I've been identifying and eating wild edibles since I was about four."

I nod. So, the two hippy-looking women are a couple. They seem exactly like the type of people who regularly cook up a pan of yard weeds for dinner. One of them—the fair-skinned woman—showed up at our house today wearing a flower crown in her hair. They look like they walked straight out of the sixties.

"My dad's been learning about that sort of thing," I say, reaching down to pick one of the weeds. "Living off the land, I mean. I think he took a class on edible plants once."

Dane smiles, and I'm caught off guard by how bright it is and how much it transforms his face. "My mom teaches that class," he says. "She takes people on a hike through the woods so they can sample all the edibles."

"Sounds like a recipe for gastrointestinal upset."

He laughs. "Only if you eat too much. Here," he adds, reaching for the chickweed stem in my hand. I let him take it, then watch as he carefully peels off the leaves. He passes one to me. "Try it."

I examine the leaf for a moment, hesitant. I've never eaten something picked from my backyard before. What if a stray cat peed there or something? I could get parasites.

Dane, seeing my reluctance, pops the rest of the leaves into his mouth like they're a handful of M&M's. I wait until he chews and swallows, and then, when he doesn't keel over, I slowly place mine on my tongue. And it tastes like...a leaf.

"Not bad, right?" Dane asks, dark eyes twinkling like he's holding back a laugh.

I force myself to swallow. "Delicious," I say, coughing a little. "Though it could use some Italian vinaigrette."

He laughs again, and I can't help smiling in response. Even though his parents are preppers and he likes to munch on weeds, he seems basically normal. I'm starting to wonder if he's preoccupied with the apocalypse like the rest of them. After all, this guy and I have something in common—an odd, unconventional something—and now might be my only chance to talk to someone who actually gets what it's like to live with a person who's actively preparing for the end of the world.

I swallow again, tasting bitterness at the back of my throat. "Are you going to Endurance Ranch?" I ask, my gaze focused on my red-painted toes peeking out from the grass.

"Oh, yeah. My parents are all over that."

The slightly wry tone in his voice surprises me, and I look up again. His good-natured smile is gone, replaced by an expression I can't quite read.

"When are you leaving?" I ask.

He shrugs and pushes his hair off his face. "The same day as everyone else, I guess. A few people from the preparedness group are leaving together, on the twenty-eighth. Isn't that when your family is going?"

The little chickweed leaf suddenly feels like an entire tree in my stomach. The twenty-eighth is only a week away. Dad said we were leaving shortly after school ended, but the actual date—coming from some guy I barely know—makes it feel more official. More inevitable.

"Yeah. The twenty-eighth." I clear the tightness from my throat. "Are you just going for a visit, or are you moving there like Dennis and Roberta?"

"We're moving there. Nick too. I think James and Kendra are just visiting, though." He looks away, his hair tumbling back over his forehead. "My moms have been packing all week. They're really excited."

"And you? What do you think about it?"

He meets my eyes again, his face still unreadable. "They're my parents. I go where they go."

Hope sparks through me. He doesn't seem excited about the ranch either. He just seems...resigned.

"I mean, it'll be great." His smile returns. "Imagine the edibles that are probably growing in Westlake Forest."

The hope fizzles again. "I think it's weird," I push back. "Like a cult or something."

Dane's expression darkens briefly, like my words flipped some imaginary switch behind his face. "I don't think there's anything weird about being prepared," he says.

The last hope sinks, and I feel a stab of disappointment. Why did I assume he was like me, forced to endure his parents' paranoia about doomsday disasters? I was so desperate to find an ally; it never occurred to me that *he* might be all in on the prepper lifestyle, too.

I change tack. "But won't you miss school and your friends?"

"Well, I'm homeschooled, so there's nothing to miss there." He looks down at the chickweed stem, still clutched in his hand. "But yeah, I'll miss my friends. How about you?"

An image of Claire, her head tipped back in laughter, pops into my head. "We're only going for a couple of weeks, so I won't have time to miss anyone."

"Oh. I thought...."

Uneasiness creeps down my spine. "You thought what?"

"Nothing. I just...." He sighs and tosses the chickweed stem into the grass. "My mom mentioned your dad is helping with construction on the new shelter."

"Yeah...."

"Well, it's just that the construction will take months, probably right into fall, so I assumed...."

Even though I'm out in the open, safe in my own backyard, my pulse starts racing like I'm trapped in a coffin that's slowly being lowered into the earth. "Did my father tell your mom that we'd be staying longer?" I ask, my tone chilly. What else does he know about my life that I don't? What else is my father keeping from me?

"I don't know," Dane says quickly. "He probably didn't tell her anything. Like I said, I just assumed."

"Well, you assumed wrong." I turn away from him, suddenly eager to get back inside to the sanctuary of my room. There's a mess to clean up, jewelry to design, a present to live. I don't have time to talk to a boy who's willing to put his fate into the hands of his doomsday prepper parents.

"Isobel."

I turn to face him again. My name sounds different coming from his mouth, familiar and new at the same time. "What?" I say, trying not to notice how attractive he looks, standing there in his perfectly fitted T-shirt, the weathered privacy fence rising up behind him.

Dane smiles again, only softly this time and without all the dazzle. "I guess I'll see you next week."

He says it like we'll be meeting up for a Sunday picnic or something, no big deal. Maybe it isn't, to him. But to me, compliance isn't the same thing as acceptance. Sometimes, all it means is that you're stuck with no other choice. Maybe I'm sticking my head in the sand against the scary realities of the world, like my mom did, but I'll never accept the ranch as a solution. She wouldn't have accepted it either.

Dane's still watching me, waiting for an answer or a nod or maybe something else altogether. Instead, I just walk away, leaving him alone by the fence.

Chapter Ten

I peer into my empty suitcase, open on my bed, and try to visualize what I'll need to pack for a survivalist ranch besides clothes. My jewelry-making supplies, for sure. A few of my favorite books. The framed picture of Mom taken at the beach the year before she died, her bare feet digging into the wet sand, the ocean deep blue and sparkling behind her. What else?

April bursts into my room, dragging her small purple suitcase and her bug-out bag behind her. She was supposed to wait for me, but apparently she started packing on her own. I can only imagine what's in there.

Twilight Sparkle is tucked into the front pocket of her bug-out bag. Seeing her favorite toy nestled among the emergency supplies makes my eyes water, and for the third time today a wave of dizziness hits me. The claustrophobic feeling has been building all week, growing stronger as each passing day brings us closer to the twenty-eighth. Now that it's just two days away, the trapped sensation is a constant pulse under my skin.

"Daddy said we're bringing these too," she says, crouching down and hooking the bug-out bag's straps over her shoulders.

She stands, the bulky bag throwing her tiny body off-balance. It's almost as big as she is. Mine is even bigger, which is why it's still in my closet, untouched until I absolutely have to move it.

"Not sure how Dad plans to fit all this stuff in the Explorer," I say, dumping underwear into my suitcase and going back for pajamas.

"You girls talking about me in here?" Dad pokes his head in my room, smiling at our progress. He's been packing all week, along with asking neighbors to pick up mail and mow the grass while we're gone. "It'll all fit," he assures me. "And if not, we can always ask Charlene and Kiana to bring something with them. They're driving out in their RV and their son's following in their car."

I pause with a pair of pajama shorts in my hand. "Dane's parents?"

He nods. "They'll be at the ranch for a couple of weeks too, then they'll stay in the RV until they find a permanent place to live. Nice people. Did you know Charlene writes for an outdoor survival magazine? And Kiana is a teacher. She moved here from Hawaii after college."

The doorbell rings, and April dashes out to answer it. Two seconds later she's running around the backyard with Rana, her packing abandoned. I stack neatly folded clothes into my suitcase while Dad goes through April's, chuckling when he realizes she's mostly packed socks and stuffed animals.

"I'll help her later," I tell him, my throat aching with held-back tears.

Dad watches me for a moment, his smile faltering. "I know this isn't what you had in mind for the summer, Isobel, but it's going to be great." His gaze lands on the framed picture of Mom, cushioned between stacks of clothes in my suitcase. "You'll see."

Then he grabs April's bug-out bag and leaves my room. Alone again, I let myself cry.

Later, after April's asleep, my father grabs the keys to the Elantra and goes outside. I watch from the living room window as he moves it into the garage. He takes Mom's car out every few days to keep the battery alive, but it's still weird to hear the engine roar to life. Mom used to hate it when Dad drove her car. *You always mess up my seat position*, she'd tell him, eyes twinkling. Then he'd say something about how it wasn't *his* fault she had short legs.

I wonder if my father remembers that. Maybe it's why he only drives her car when he absolutely has to.

By the time Dad comes back inside, I'm sitting in my room, packed suitcase still open on the bed beside me. When I hear the shower, I slip out of my room and quietly make my way to the garage, grabbing the car keys from their hook in the kitchen on the way.

The garage is pitch-dark. I flick on the light, wincing at the sudden brightness. The Elantra takes up most of the space, Dad's tools and planks of wood all pushed up against the walls. I unlock the doors, then climb into the driver's seat.

The car is still warm from sitting in the sun all day, so I leave the door open a crack. The scents of lumber and motor oil filter in, mingling with the stale air. I grip the steering wheel and breathe in, trying—as I always do—to recapture a hint of the old shampoo-and-hand-sanitizer smell. But it's really gone, so instead I try to remember the last time my mother ever sat where I'm sitting.

It would have been a couple of months before she died. She was determined to keep going, just keep living, for as long as she could. She went to work, even though she was tired and thin and sick from all the drugs being pumped into her. She drove April to daycare. She drove me to school, though I kept insisting she didn't have to. But she wanted the mundane tasks. She wanted to live in the moment with us, even through the exhaustion and pain. She must have known what was coming—as a nurse, she knew about the low survival rate of pancreatic cancer—but she refused to focus on the end when there was still so much left to experience in the present.

My phone rings in my sweater pocket, jerking me back to my own present. It's my godmother Traci.

"Hi, Traci," I say, instantly concerned. She doesn't usually call so late.

"Hey, sweets. What's new with you? How did finals go?"

Finals. Right. School feels like ages ago. "Fine," I say. I almost add *considering what's been going on*, but something stops me.

"Glad to hear it." Traci clears her throat. "So, I spoke to April earlier."

"April?" I sit up straight. "When?"

"A couple of hours ago. She answered your dad's phone when I called."

"Oh." Dad often leaves his phone inside when he's puttering around in the garage, which he was doing after dinner.

"She mentioned something about you guys visiting a ranch?"

I freeze, my hand clenched on my phone. Of course April told her about the ranch. She's been telling everyone within hearing distance about how she's going on a road trip to ride horses and hike in the woods. No one has any idea that this ranch is actually a survival community, because April doesn't know herself.

"Oh," I repeat, my mouth suddenly dry.

"I tried calling your dad again to ask him about it, but he's not picking up." Her tone, while still upbeat, has an unmistakable layer of concern underneath. "So I'm asking you."

Now's my chance. I can tell Traci everything. The bug-out bags, the preparedness group, the bunker blueprint, Endurance Ranch...everything. Maybe she can stop this. Talk some sense into Dad. Prevent him, somehow, from getting April and me mixed up in his doomsday lifestyle. Maybe even intervene and take us away.

Is that what I want? April and I have each other, but Dad only has us. Telling Traci would be like starting a boulder rolling down a hill. Once it veers out of my control, there's no going back.

During my fight with Dad, when I threatened to tell Traci about the ranch, I was so sure I could do it. But now, with the perfect chance right in front of me, I can't make myself say the words. I'm too much of a coward.

"It's nothing." I keep my voice light even though my heart is thumping so loud I'm afraid she'll hear it through the phone. "Dad mentioned possibly visiting this ranch nearby where people can ride horses and stuff. April's a bit obsessed. You know how she is about horses."

There's a long pause as Traci takes this in. Beads of sweat form on my forehead as I wait for her to respond. I hate lying, not to mention I suck at it.

"Okay," she says, finally, not sounding overly convinced. "I just thought I'd ask."

"Of course." Suddenly I'm desperate to get off the phone before she extracts the truth out of me anyway. "Listen, I'm kind of in the middle of—"

"Promise me something, Isobel."

I swallow. "What?"

"Promise you'll call me if you ever need anything. Support, help, my recipe for key lime cheesecake, anything."

"Your key lime cheesecake *is* amazing," I say, relaxing a little.

"And I want you to know that you're welcome to visit us anytime," she goes on in the same serious tone. "Just say the word. Our door is always open for you."

"I know." She says this, or something similar, during almost every phone call. But this time, the words sound different. Like she really needs me to hear them.

"Promise me," she says again.

I think about Traci and Heath's house, a cute brick bungalow I've only seen in pictures. It's far from here—a four-day drive—but only five hours from the ranch. Then I think about the car I'm currently sitting in, completely useless to me since I'm not legally allowed to drive by myself.

Our door is always open for you. A lot of good that does me if I can't get there.

"I promise," I reply anyway.

We hang up, and I sit in the silence for a few minutes. I reach up and tap the purple ribbon pendant hanging off the rearview mirror, making it swing. The thick black cord it's attached to slides forward with the force, and I catch a glimpse of something else, something I haven't noticed before now. A glint of silver that looks vaguely familiar.

My heart squeezes like a fist when I realize what it is. Gently, I move the black cord aside and hook my finger around the sterling silver chain bracelet, looking for the heart-shaped charm I'd attached to one of the links. I was ten years old, brand new to jewelry-making, and I'd been so proud to present this piece to my mom on her birthday. She loved it, promising to never take it off. And she kept her promise until the toggle clasp broke off a couple years later. I'd assumed she'd lost it. How had I never noticed it here? I have no idea when she'd threaded a piece of string between the end links and hung it on her rearview mirror.

I turn the charm over, running my thumb over the six letters stamped into the silver-plated pewter. *Always.* A reference to the words she used to say to me at bedtime when I was little, right before she turned out the light: *Love you always.* The same words I whispered to her the day she died.

The letters blur. I wipe my tears away and get out of the car, grabbing an X-Acto knife from my dad's toolbox. Back in the driver's seat, I run the blade over the bracelet's connecting string, then catch it in my palm as it falls free.

When I confronted Dad after his conversation with Dennis in the garage, he told me I was like my mom, unwilling to see the big picture. *She assumed the world would always be here. She assumed she'd always be here, too.*

She was wrong about the second thing—and possibly the first thing too—but at least she never stopped believing that everything would turn out okay.

Chapter Eleven

The sun is still low in the sky when we pull into the Starbucks parking lot, the pre-arranged meeting spot for the Weldon Preparedness Group members heading to Endurance Ranch. As Dad parks the Explorer, I spot red-haired Nick a few spaces down, standing in front of a grungy Jeep Wrangler and sipping from a Starbucks cup, a large German shepherd at his side. The dog starts barking the moment we step out of the car, which might worry me if I didn't already feel like I swallowed a box of thumbtacks.

I carefully maneuver April away from the dog and into the Starbucks, more to get away for a moment than anything else. Food is the last thing my churning stomach wants.

When we get back outside, Dad, Nick, and his dog are standing in front of an ancient-looking Winnebago that's taking up at least three spots at the back of the lot. As April and I head toward them, blueberry muffins and steaming coffees in our hands, the door of the Winnebago swings open and Dane's dark-haired mom steps out, followed by his blond one. I expect Dane to appear next, but then

I see him a few spots away, climbing out of a small red Volkswagen.

Right. Dad mentioned that Dane's parents were driving to the ranch in their RV while Dane took the car. Looking at that Winnebago, though, I'll be surprised if it makes it a hundred miles, let alone two thousand.

"Thanks, hon," my father says when I hand him his coffee, strong and black, the way he likes it.

"Who else are we waiting on?" Dane's blond mom—Charlene—asks the group.

Nick checks his watch. "Just James and Kendra. Gail and Stuart are flying out in a few weeks."

"Flying," Dad repeats. "They don't want to have their vehicle out there with them?"

Nick shakes his head. "They said they're selling everything and starting over fresh."

Even though the sun is now beating down on us, I shiver. Gail and Stuart are the old white-haired couple, I think. I can't imagine wanting to spend your retirement hundreds of miles away from home, stuck in an unfamiliar town while you wait for the world to crumble.

Quietly, I step a few feet away from the group and take out my phone. I know Claire's probably not awake yet, but I send her a text anyway. *Leaving soon. I'll update you as often as I can.*

To my surprise, a response arrives less than a minute later. *Yes please. Heading to camp tomorrow morning, which means limited access to my phone, but I'll check in whenever I have time and Wi-Fi.*

Sounds good. I'll miss you.

I'll miss you too. ☹ Be careful, Iz. Love you. Text me when you stop for the night.

I will. Love you too. ☁

I pocket my phone and look over at April, who's standing next to Dad and devouring her blueberry muffin with single-minded focus. Remembering the latte in my hand, I take my first sip, realizing immediately that I shouldn't have asked for that extra squirt of syrup. The sharp sweetness is enough to make my eyes water, but I need to put something in my stomach before we leave, and the caffeine jolt is welcome after my night of broken sleep.

"Is that hazelnut?"

I turn around to see Dane, sitting on the hood of the Volkswagen a few feet away. "What?"

He motions toward my Starbucks cup with his hand, and I notice he's wearing the hemp bracelet again. "I can smell it from here. Hazelnut's my favorite."

My gaze drops to my cup for a moment before drifting back up to him. In his light gray shorts, faded blue T-shirt, and dark sunglasses, he looks like he's ready to spend the day lounging on the beach instead of driving on the highway.

"Yeah, it's hazelnut," I say, moving a few steps closer. "Are you trying to tell me that you want a sip? You still have time to get one of your own, you know."

Dane's eyebrows shoot up over the edge of his sunglasses, and I realize my words came out a little snootier than I'd intended.

"Nah." He folds his tanned arms across his chest. "My parents would kill me if they saw me with a Starbucks cup in my hand. Most of their coffee isn't fair trade, and big chains like them put the little mom-and-pop places out of business."

I glance down at my latte with a tinge of guilt. "Oh."

"I still go, though," he says, dropping his voice so only I can hear. "When they're not around. I love the white chocolate mocha Frappuccinos."

Something inside me perks up at this. Sneaking forbidden Frappuccinos is such a simple act of rebellion, but it's enough to show me that maybe he doesn't agree with his parents about everything.

"Me too," I say, taking a big gulp of my latte.

James and Kendra—the young couple with the baby—pull up in a shiny new SUV. Nick's dog starts barking again, inciting a startled cry from baby Micah, who'd been dozing in his mom's arms. Nick tries to calm the dog while James and Kendra soothe the baby, and the complete chaos is like a preview of how the next few days are probably going to go. My head throbs, either from the noise or the straight shot of sugar I just injected into my bloodstream.

"Okay, guys," Nick calls out once everyone is finally settled. "Let's go over the itinerary again."

I meet Dane's eyes, my heart suddenly lodged in my throat. This is it. Everyone is here and accounted for. Nothing left to stop us from leaving. Dane doesn't seem to notice my panic. He lets out a jaw-cracking yawn and slowly pushes off the car. How can he be so calm? He's leaving his home and moving to a place he's never been, filled with people he doesn't know. I'm only leaving for a couple of weeks and I'm terrified.

We join the rest of the group gathered around Nick. Clearly, he stepped into Dennis's shoes after he left.

"As we discussed at our last meeting...." Nick pauses and reaches into the pocket of his cargo shorts, bringing out a folded sheet of paper. He smooths it open. "We're aiming to do five hundred miles a day, so that should get us to the ranch by Monday night. If anyone wants to push through to get there a day earlier, they're welcome to." He squints down at the sheet. "Tonight's rest stop is the Hearthstone Motel in Briarwood. Everyone has their room booked, right?"

Dad, James, and Kendra all nod, while Charlene pats the side of the Winnebago. "We'll probably stay at a nearby campground with old Winnie here," she says.

"Unless the weather is exceptionally hot or rainy," Kiana adds. "In that case, we'll stay at the motel. There's no air conditioning in this thing and the roof leaks when it rains."

Charlene smiles and rolls her eyes. "Out of the two of us, it's the native Hawaiian who's bothered by heat and water. Go figure."

Kiana elbows her playfully. "Shush."

Nick puts the itinerary back in his pocket and reaches into the Jeep, bringing out a map. He unfolds it and spreads it out on the hood. "I figure we'll just stick to the highway. That'll get us to Briarwood by early evening."

Dad takes a sip of coffee, wincing at either the temperature or the taste. "You know," he says, leaning over the open map, "if we get off on Exit 27 and take Springer Road instead of the highway, we could be there an hour earlier. That route shaves off seventy miles." He runs a finger along the map to illustrate.

Nick frowns. "I don't think so, Gabe. The highway keeps it simple."

"Well, there's a road toll here." Dad taps at a spot. "We could avoid that if we go Springer Road. I know the route; I've taken it before. It's definitely quicker."

"I know the route too," Nick says, his fair skin reddening. "I was a long-haul truck driver for twelve years, remember?"

Dad steps back and takes another drink. He doesn't wince this time.

"How about this," Charlene pipes up. "Those who want to go the highway can go the highway, and those who want to go the alternate route can go the alternate route. Problem solved."

"I think we should try to stick together," Kendra says, jiggling baby Micah. "What if someone has an accident or... vehicle trouble?" She glances at the Winnebago as she utters this last part, and Kiana shoots her a grin.

"Exactly," Nick says, refolding the map.

"So let's *all* take Springer Road," James put in. "I like the idea of cutting off an hour and dodging the toll."

Everyone murmurs their agreement. Everyone except for Nick, whose face gets even redder. I get the feeling he doesn't like being challenged.

"Fine," he says tonelessly. "We'll do it Gabe's way."

I peek over at my father to gauge his reaction, but he doesn't look smug or triumphant. That's not his way.

"Anyway, moving on." Nick clears his throat and straightens his ratty baseball cap. "We'll keep in touch over text, and if something comes up, car trouble or whatever, let someone know. And that's basically it." He tosses the map back in the Jeep. "Safe travels, everyone."

There's a general hum of excitement as the group disperses. April darts ahead of me, heading toward the car, and I quickly catch up and take her hand. Dane walks past and grins at me. "See you there," he says.

Flustered by both his smile and his nonchalant attitude, I turn away without responding. Dad's already sitting in the driver's seat, the radio tuned in to the nineties rock station he likes.

"Ready?" he asks once we're both buckled in.

"Ready!" April shouts from the back.

Again, I don't say a word as the Explorer starts zipping steadily along the highway. Everyone else seems eager to get started on this exciting new adventure, while I'm a prickly ball of doubt and anxiety. I wish I could just brush myself off and keep going, like my mother always taught me, but there's no getting rid of this feeling. The further we get from home, the tighter it grips.

Chapter Twelve

The next two days pass in a blur of gas stations, dingy motels, and greasy fast food. April sleeps for hours at a time, clutching her stuffed crocodile with one hand. I sleep sometimes too, but lightly, dozing on and off as I listen to music or an audiobook on my phone. Most of the time I stare out the window, watching the trees and small towns go by and wishing I was anywhere else besides on this highway, stuck in this car.

When Dad's not listening to his dreary nineties music—what my mother used to refer to as *grunge*—he has the radio tuned into a news station for the weather forecast. We don't talk much aside from discussing where to stop or whether we'd rather air conditioning or open windows.

Sometimes I forget, just for a moment or two, about where we're going. We could be on any road trip, heading wherever, listening to music as the scenery passes. But the moment never lasts.

"You can change the station, if you want."

My father's voice startles me out of my trance. "No, it's okay," I say, arching my stiff back.

It's our third day on the road. One more night in a motel, one more full day of driving tomorrow, and we'll be at the ranch. I close my eyes and try not to think about it.

I'm just starting to doze off again when the sky turns dark and a large raindrop hits the windshield. Then another. Seconds later, we drive into a torrential downpour, water pounding against the car like we're in a giant carwash. Dad lets out a soft curse and slows down.

"What's happening?" April says groggily from the back seat.

"It's nothing," I say, turning to smile at her. "Just some heavy rain."

My words are punctuated by a deafening crash of thunder that sounds like it's coming from directly above us. All three of us jump, and Dad slows the car to a crawl as the rain thrashes against the windows. The world outside disappears into the downpour. In the distance, a bolt of lightning cuts through the sky, instantly followed by another crack of thunder.

"I'm pulling over," Dad says in a strained voice. He flicks on his blinker and pulls to the side of the highway, then puts on the hazard lights. Through the sheets of rain ahead of us, I can just make out another car doing the same.

"Are we going to get hit by lightning?" April asks, fully awake now.

"No, probably not," Dad says, his hands tight on the wheel. He lets go for a second to turn up the radio, but all we hear is an ad for a mattress store. "We're safest in here because if lightning did hit us, most of the current would flow around the car and into the ground. I'm more concerned about...." His voice trails off and he peers out the window, frantically scanning the sky.

"More concerned about what?" I ask, the words almost drowned out as the raindrops turn to hail. Little white blobs ping off the windshield and hood, making me feel like we're literally being attacked by nature. My heart thrums along with the rain, and for a moment, I almost understand why Dad's so fearful.

"Tornados," Dad replies as he watches the clouds. "They're much more common in this part of the country."

"Tornados?" April repeats in a high-pitched voice.

"Don't worry." I stick my arm between the seats and offer her my hand. She takes it, then loops her other arm around her stuffed crocodile toy, like she's comforting it as much as herself. "There's no sign of any tornados."

I glance at Dad, hoping for confirmation on this, but he's still on the lookout for funnel clouds.

A few minutes later the hail stops, returning to plain old rain. That slows down too, and the next boom of thunder is just a rumble in the distance. I let go of my sister's hand.

We wait another ten minutes to be sure the storm is passing, then Dad turns off the hazard lights, starts the engine, and slowly pulls back onto the drenched road. His hands, I notice, are trembling slightly on the wheel, and his face is pale and sweaty.

"Are you okay?" I say it quietly so April won't hear me and get concerned.

He lets out a breath and nods, his gaze steady on the road. "I'll feel even better when we get to the ranch. The structures there were built to withstand all types of weather, so at least we won't have to worry about getting flattened by a freak storm this summer."

My pulse thuds like it's giving off a warning. "This summer," I repeat, frowning. "Don't you mean for the next two weeks? That's how long we're staying, right?"

He doesn't answer for a moment, focusing instead on passing the slow minivan in front of us. Once we're safely on the other side again, he glances at me, his expression blank. "Right."

I've managed to make it through this entire drive so far without feeling trapped, but it's building now as I stare at my father's profile. I turn away and open the window a crack, letting in the warm breeze, but even that doesn't do much to soothe me. The air is different here, just like everything else. The farther away we get, the more disconnected I feel, both from myself and from everything I left behind.

Tonight's motel is much like the first two, old and utilitarian and in the ass end of nowhere. All the other vehicles are there when we pull in, even the Winnebago. For once we're the last to arrive, probably because we stopped so long to wait out the storm.

"Hey, McCarthys!"

James, Charlene, Nick, and the dog—whose name, I discovered, is Max—are standing in a loose circle near the motel office. Dad waves and the three of us head in their direction.

"Did you get caught in the rain too, Gabe?" Charlene asks when we reach them.

Dad nods. "The storm passed right over us."

"It missed us completely," James says. "We must have been ahead of it."

Nick gives Max a scratch behind the ears. "It passed right over me too. Did you see that lightning? Good thing I have my Faraday cage in the Jeep."

"During a thunderstorm, your car acts like a Faraday cage," Dad says matter-of-factly.

Pink blotches appear on Nick's pale neck. "I know. But it doesn't hurt to have extra protection."

"Hey, so," Charlene's cheerful voice cuts through the tension, "the rest of us decided that we want something resembling real food for dinner, so we're thinking of heading to a little town a few miles down the road. They've *got* to have a restaurant that serves vegetables or beans."

"Sounds good," Dad says as April makes a face, horrified by the idea of eating vegetables on a road trip.

"Let's meet back here in twenty minutes," Nick says before turning away, Max at his heels. Charlene and James wander off too, leaving the three of us to check in.

"Ready?" Dad asks after we've all taken turns freshening up in the miniscule bathroom. The room smells a bit like stale smoke, though the place has apparently been smoke-free for years. At this point, an underground shelter is starting to sound appealing.

"Um," I say, hanging back. "I think I'm going to pass on the restaurant. I'm not really hungry."

Dad frowns. "You sure?"

I nod. After eight hours in the car, the last thing I want to do is get back in it, even for a few minutes. All I want is an hour to myself, in a stationary space, without music or talking or holding my bladder. I actually *am* hungry, but I'm craving solitude more than food right now. Besides, there has to be somewhere to get food around this place.

After Dad and April leave, I text Claire to let her know I'm still alive. She's probably running around a soccer field and won't answer until later tonight, but I feel better just texting her. Our little check-in messages are the only thing keeping me tethered to home.

After that, I'm not sure what to do with myself. I try to watch TV, but the motel has crappy reception and limited options, so I give up and go outside for a walk. I've done more than enough sitting for one day, anyway.

Since the motel is on a busy road with nothing else for miles, my walking space is pretty much restricted to the parking lot. I make the best of it, walking the perimeter and then cutting through the center, enjoying the late evening sun on my skin.

As I stroll past the front of the Winnebago, I notice that both the outer door and the screen are wide open. I pause, looking around. The Volkswagen is gone, so I assumed they all went to dinner. Unless....

My suspicions are confirmed when Dane appears in the open doorway, holding a blue towel. "Oh, hey," he says when he spots me. He shakes out the towel, which has damp patches all over it.

"What are you doing?" I ask.

"The roof leaked pretty bad during the rainstorm," he replies, tossing the wet towel back inside. "I'm trying to dry out the sleeping areas so we can stay in it tonight, but I don't think that's happening."

I step a little closer. "You skipped dinner at a restaurant for this?" It hasn't escaped my attention that during every preparedness meeting I've witnessed so far, Dane has spent most of the time outside of it. For someone who balked at my insinuation that the group is almost cult-like, he sure doesn't seem too interested in being involved.

Dane presses his hands on either side of the door and leans out. "I volunteered. Someone had to air this thing out. Besides, I'm not much of a people person. Why aren't *you* with the rest of the group?"

"Because I'm not part of the group."

He doesn't look surprised at this. "So you don't believe in preparing for TEOTWAWKI?"

"Tia what?"

"T-E-O-T-W-A-W-K-I," he spells out. "The end of the world as we know it."

"Oh," I say, feeling dumb. The daughter of a doomsday prepper should probably know all the acronyms. "I just think there's such a thing as going too far."

"And you think the ranch is going too far," Dane says, looking right at me. His eyes are dark, dark brown, his pupils almost blending in with the rest of the iris.

My stomach quivers but not entirely from lack of food. "It *is* a bit extreme, don't you think? I mean, I get why people would want to prepare for some things. The world is really scary with the economy and climate change and everything. But there has to be a better way to fight back than holing up in the woods and waiting for something bad to happen. Instead of preparing for the end of the world, wouldn't it make more sense to, you know, put all that energy into trying to fix it?"

Right then, my stomach decides to let out a loud, monstrous growl. Dane raises his eyebrows.

"I was just about to make a peanut butter sandwich," he says, dropping his arms. "You interested?"

I definitely am. Still, I hesitate, unsure how wise it would be to step into a confined space with a guy I barely know, while all the adults are miles away lingering over a hot meal. But Dane seems decent, and we *are* still in public, sort of, so I think it'll be okay. And I'm starving.

"Sure," I say. Dane moves aside, and I climb into the RV.

The interior reminds me of the pictures I've seen of my parents' childhood homes. Shaggy beige carpeting on the floor, brown paneling on the walls and cabinets, an ancient microwave above the tiny stove, flowery wallpaper in the kitchen nook. It smells exactly like it looks—old, damp, and musty.

"Classy, right?" Dane smiles and holds out his arms, like he's presenting me with a prize. "It used to belong to my grandparents. They bought it brand new in 1985."

"Wow," I say, crossing my arms. "Vintage."

"That's one word for it." He turns to the kitchen area and opens one of the cabinets, removing a loaf of bread and a jar of peanut butter. The brands and packaging aren't familiar—they look like the kinds of products you'd see in the organic section of the supermarket—but I'm not picky.

I watch Dane assemble two sandwiches, stirring the oily peanut butter with a spoon before spreading it on the seed-filled bread. He cuts the finished sandwiches in half and transfers them to two plates, then leans down to open the tiny fridge.

"Sorry, we just have almond milk," he says, looking over his shoulder at me. "Both my moms are vegan."

"Water is fine."

He pours two glasses of water from the tap and hands mine to me along with my sandwich. Then we sit on the threadbare futon/sofa, which I assume is his bed when he sleeps in here.

"Are you vegan too?" I ask, biting into my sandwich. It isn't Skippy on white bread, but I'm too hungry to care.

"No. Vegetarian is as far as I'm willing to go."

His wording makes it sound like a life of vegetarianism wasn't entirely his choice. I decide to dig a little deeper.

"So, what about you?" I ask. "What do you think about teot-whatever?"

He laughs. "TEOTWAWKI. I don't know," he says with a shrug. "This is all I've ever known. This lifestyle, preparing for the end. I grew up learning how to survive in case of food shortages or a government takeover. My parents don't trust the government." He laughs again but then sighs. "They don't trust anyone, really. Except for each other and me and the people in the preparedness group."

"But what do *you* think?" I ask again.

He's quiet for a moment. "I have my own beliefs. Some match theirs, and some don't." He shrugs again, something he does a lot, I've noticed. "But they're my family, you know? I go where they go."

He said the same thing in my yard, but the resignation in his tone doesn't spark hope in me like it did then. Now it just bothers me. "Are you always this passive?"

A slight flush rises in his face and he shakes his head, smiling. "Are you always this blunt?"

"No, but I'd like to be."

We avoid looking at each other as we eat the last of our sandwiches in silence, then I get up to leave. "Thanks for dinner," I say, placing my dishes in the miniature sink.

"You're welcome," he says. "And by the way...." He's staring down at his empty plate, like he's looking for the right words hidden in the crumbs. "I'm not passive. I just believe in picking my battles."

I frown, struggling to make sense of his reaction. Why does he care what I think of him? I'm just a person he's traveling with, the daughter of his parents' friend, a girl who doesn't even want to be here.

"Well, this feels like a pretty big battle to me," I reply.

A car door slams outside, followed by voices and the now-familiar sounds of Max's barks and baby Micah crying.

"See you tomorrow," I say, taking one more look around this eighties time capsule before stepping back out into the present.

Chapter Thirteen

When Dad's phone alarm jars me awake the next morning, I feel like I barely slept at all.

I crack open one eye, my mind still half-trapped in fragmented dreams. The room is dark, a strip of muted light visible through the heavy curtains. My father sits on the other bed, fully dressed, his face lit up by his phone screen. April is splayed out across the mattress, one arm thrown over my torso. I spent the night tossing and turning, worrying about today and where we'll be at the end of it.

"We're outta here in forty-five minutes, girls," he says softly. "Breakfast on the road today."

That heartens me. At least I don't have to sit around with the Weldon Preparedness Group, trying to squeeze food past my tight throat as they talk excitedly about the ranch. The pit in my stomach is already big enough.

I can't, however, avoid them in the motel parking lot. When April and I emerge from the room a half hour later, both of us groggy and yawning, the entire group has assembled near Nick's Jeep. Nick is holding court as usual, Max sitting beside him.

"Does everyone have their maps?" he's saying as we sidle up next to Dad. "The ranch is a bit of a challenge to locate, for obvious reasons. Have your map at hand so you know exactly which roads to take."

The group, looking as weary and haggard after three days on the road as we undoubtedly do, nods in unison. I peek across the semicircle at Dane, who's standing between his parents and staring off into the distance. As if he senses my eyes on him, he meets my gaze and smiles. After I left the Winnebago last night, I wondered if I'd offended him with my bluntness. That doesn't seem to be the case. I give him a small smile back and look away.

"The management definitely knows we're coming, right?" Kendra asks, biting her lip as she hugs the baby close to her chest. Micah grabs one of her braids and cheerfully stuffs it in his mouth, oblivious to the air of nervous excitement.

"Yes," Nick assures her. "I spoke to Dennis last night. They know when to expect us."

He stands up a little straighter as he says this, like we all should be impressed that Dennis clearly chose *him* as his outside contact and right-hand man. I quickly roll my eyes, unable to contain myself, but then I realize Dane is still watching me, a small, bemused smile on his lips. Flustered, I look at the ground.

"You spoke to Dennis?" Charlene asks eagerly. "How's he doing? How's Roberta?"

Nick smiles, pleased again. "Yeah, he called me." He looks like he's going to say more, but then Dad cuts in.

"They're doing fine. He called me too, before we left. They're fitting in well."

Nick's expression hardens and then the blotches appear, the redness creeping up his neck to his cheeks. That tense silence descends again, making everyone fidget and avert their eyes from Nick's patchwork face. Well, everyone but Dad, who appears unaffected by the awkwardness.

"Right," Nick says. He clears his throat and looks away from my father, focusing instead on the women. "They're looking forward to seeing us. Dennis says the property is beautiful and the pictures on the website don't do it justice."

Charlene and Kiana smile at each other. How can they be excited? I want to scream *This isn't a real summer vacation!* at everyone. We're not heading to a resort to drink piña coladas on the beach while we work on our tans. We're going to visit a survival community that's designed to save us from the theoretical end of the world. There's nothing fun or exciting about it.

"I'll call Dennis when we get close, so he can be there to verify who we are," Nick continues. "If we just showed up unexpectedly, we wouldn't get past the guard. Dennis said the security is strict, even during noncrisis periods. But it needs to be, you know, for everyone's safety."

"Sounds like we're going to a prison," I say.

Everyone turns to look at me, and heat floods my face. I didn't mean to say it so loud—didn't mean to say it at all, actually—but the words just tumbled out, propelled by the swell of panic in my chest.

"Isobel," my father says, his voice low and reproachful.

"Prison." Nick turns his cold eyes on me and gives a derisive laugh. "I've never heard of a prison that has a farm and horses and a shooting range, have you?"

Everyone laughs with him, except for Dane, who looks sympathetic, and Dad, who doesn't look at me at all. A burning pressure builds behind my eyes, and I turn and walk away before anyone can notice. The only place I can escape to is the car. I lean against the bumper, facing away from the group. Then I take out my phone, pretending that's the real reason I came over here.

Surprisingly, I *do* have a text. It's from Claire, sent late last night but just delivered this morning. *Yo! I miss you. How's it going?*

Just seeing her name is enough to release the logjam of tears. I blink them away as I type back my response: *I want to go home.*

↙

My father waits until April dozes off in her booster seat sometime after lunch before bringing up this morning's incident.

"You compared the ranch to a prison, Isobel." He turns down the stereo and frowns at me. "How can you think that?"

"Guards, security, isolation from society...that's like the definition of a prison, Dad. How can I *not* think that?"

"It's not a prison if you're free to go at any time," he fires back. "The members aren't *locked* in there, you know."

"I saw the website; I know how it works. The whole *point* is that the members *are* locked in there, so the marauders or whatever can't ambush them." I put air quotes around *marauders* to show him how ridiculous all this sounds, like the plot of a postapocalyptic TV show.

"What I mean is," he says with deliberate calm, "unless an emergency happens, we can come and go as we please. Unlike prisoners, we're *choosing* to be there."

"*You're* choosing to be there *for* us." I yank my seatbelt away from my body, loosening it. I'm so sick of being in this car. Sick of the endless highways and the gas station peanuts and the blur of trees out my window. Sick of the constant sinking feeling. "April and I didn't choose any of this."

He glances between the road and my face, his eyes wide like he's surprised, even though I've expressed my opinion several times already. Maybe he wasn't really listening before. Or maybe he's just hearing my desperation, which grows stronger the closer we get.

"I'm doing this for you," he says, his tone laced with hurt. "You and April. The world is a pressure cooker right now, and someday soon, it's going to blow. Maybe you're too young to grasp the potential devastation of that—"

"You think I'm too young to grasp the devastation?" I say, my voice wobbling. "I watched Mom waste away to nothing and then die. *That* was devastating, and it made me grow up pretty fast. So I think I understand how bad things can get."

Dad's face goes pale, his fingers tightening on the wheel. We never talk about the day Mom died. We were both there when it happened, standing beside her bed as she took her last breath and quietly drifted away. Afterward, a nurse came in to remove the tubes from her body and shut off all the machines. I'll never forget the cold, eerie silence.

I understand what the worst looks like.

"We need to take control," Dad says after a pause.

Take control. It's what Dennis said to him that night I overheard them in the garage, a few days before he left for the ranch. *We need to take control of our situation.*

"You can't control everything," I bite out. "Mom knew that more than anyone. Even full of cancer, she knew there's only so much you can do to avoid the worst-case scenario. She *never* would've agreed to this trip and you know it."

Color returns to his face in scarlet blotches. "Well, she's not here anymore, is she, so it's all up to me. I have to take care of you both now, and this is the best way I know how. I'm sorry your mom isn't here, but that's the way it is. It's about time you accepted this, Isobel."

"I won't ever accept what you're doing."

"I'm protecting you. If you can't—"

"Why are you yelling?" April's voice, thick with sleep, filters into the front seat, and the tense mood changes abruptly. My father and I disagree about a lot of things, but protecting April is a top priority for both of us. There's a long beat of silence, both of us trying to control our anger. "Are we almost at the ranch?" she asks.

"Not long now, Sunshine," Dad says, giving her a forced smile in the rearview. He grabs the sheet of paper he'd stuck between his seat and the middle console, then hands it back to her. "Why don't you find it for us on the map?"

This will keep her busy for a few minutes. I lean back, close my eyes, and try to calm myself down. Exhausted, I let the sounds around me fade away, and my mind goes blissfully blank as I gradually fall into sleep.

I'm jostled into consciousness again when the car hits a giant bump in the road. I blink and look at the clock—5:14—then at the rural landscape outside my window. We left the highway at some point, and now we're driving on a narrow, two-lane road, a thick line of trees on either side of us.

"Where are we?" I ask, rubbing my eyes.

"Helm Road," Dad says, his gaze locked straight ahead. "About twenty miles east of Westlake Forest."

My stomach flips. We're almost there. I turn to look at April, who's busy playing a game on her tablet, her crocodile nestled in her lap.

"Isobel."

My father's face is flushed, and that familiar gleam is back in his eyes, a mix of anxiety and excitement. His ranch expression. "What?"

"Just promise me you'll give this place a chance."

Instead of responding, I let the silence hang between us like a curtain. Outside my window there's nothing to see but trees and one lone crow, soaring through the sky above the road. I follow the bird's progress, black wings wide as it glides toward the treetops and then disappears from view.

I'm starting to wonder if this road goes on forever when we make a sharp turn onto a narrow gravel road. Dad slows down and quickly rechecks the map, I guess to make sure we're not heading into hunting ground or someone's private property.

"This is spooky," April says as a tree branch scrapes the side of the car.

I agree—the tall trees are blocking out the sun, making it almost as dark as night, and we seem to be the only vehicle for miles. If we broke down here, we'd either get lost or eaten by wildlife or both.

Just as I'm wondering if *this* road goes on forever, the trees thin out to reveal a large clearing scattered with log buildings, rows of crops, and shiny black solar panels, soaking up the last of the sun. There are no signs to identify it, but since we're surrounded by woods with nothing else for miles, this has to be the place.

Endurance Ranch.

Chapter Fourteen

The first person we see is a tall blond guy standing near a crude, wooden archway that appears to mark the entrance to the main residential area. He's dressed casually in jeans and a T-shirt, and so far as I can see, he's unarmed. I don't know what I was expecting—a tough military type in camo, maybe?—but I'm relieved we aren't being greeted at gunpoint.

The man watches our car as we approach, his expression firm and cautious, then he lifts one hand, motioning for us to stop. My pulse thuds as Dad hits the brakes and rolls down his window.

"Good evening," the blond guy says, leaning down to see inside the car. As he does, I notice the design on the top left of his shirt. A jaguar head inside a circle—the Endurance Ranch logo. "Where are you folks coming from?"

Dad tells him, then adds, "I'm Gabe McCarthy, and these are my daughters. Is Dennis here?"

The wariness fades from the guy's face and he smiles. "My apologies for stopping you. Dennis said you were arriving today, but I just wanted to make sure." He straightens up and gestures behind him. "Go on up. You can park your car beside the lodge. That's the big log building with the blue door."

Dad thanks him, and we inch forward again, driving under the arch and up a slight incline toward the log buildings. We're silent as we take in the scenery. Westlake Forest stretches out before us, so vast and thick that it feels like it must go on forever. I spot a crow perched on an old, grizzled pine tree and wonder if it's the same one I was watching earlier.

We find the lodge without any issues, and Dad parks in the gravel lot beside it. Nick's Jeep is parked a few feet away, but no one else from our convoy seems to be here yet.

"Wow," my father says as we climb out of the car. He sucks in the fresh, piney air and looks around. "The pictures on the website really don't do it justice."

I look around too, my overwhelmed brain taking everything in. The big two-story lodge, its porch lined with flowerpots. The scattering of log cabins at the edge of the forest. A covered wooden gazebo, situated on a platform of rocks overlooking the vast expanse of land in the distance. It feels surreal, like I'm still in the car, asleep against the window, and trapped in a dream I can't seem to wake up from.

"I need to use the bathroom," April says, and just like that I'm back in reality.

Dad takes her hand, and we head toward the lodge. Just as we reach the steps, the blue door opens and Nick emerges, followed by Dennis and a balding man with glasses. Dennis spots us first, and his face breaks into a huge grin.

"Gabe," he says as he walks down the stairs, his arm already extended for a handshake. "It's so good to see you all here. Hey, girls," he says to April and me. I notice he's sporting the ranch logo too, only his is stitched above the pocket of his button-down shirt. "How was your trip? Are you excited to finally be here?"

"I need to use the bathroom," April repeats, unimpressed.

"Oh, of course." He laughs and motions for us to go ahead inside, like he owns the place even though he's only been here for a few weeks. "I'm sure we can rustle you up something to eat too. You guys must be hungry."

On the porch, Nick and the balding man are engrossed in a conversation. As we pass, the man turns to greet us. "You must be the McCarthys. Gabe, Isobel, and April, right? I've heard a lot about you from Dennis."

Dad pauses to shake his hand too, but I hang back. Who is this guy?

"This is Russell," Dennis answers my unspoken question. He grips the man's shoulder with his large hand. "He's the CEO of Endurance Ranch."

I try to keep the surprise from my face. I'm not sure what shocks me more—that a survival ranch has a CEO or that this guy is it. I expected someone big and commanding, maybe, like Dennis. Certainly not this guy, with his gaunt features, thick glasses, and pressed khaki shirt. He looks more like a high school math teacher.

Beside me, April wiggles like she's got ants in her pants, a sure sign that she's a minute or so away from an accident. Dennis notices and quickly ushers us into the lodge.

The interior of the place is set up like an open-concept house, with the living room, kitchen, and dining room all situated in one large, airy room. Virtually everything is made of wood—floors, walls, cabinets, furniture, the spiral staircase to the second floor. It's like a lumberyard exploded in here.

Dennis shows us where the bathroom is, and I tag along with April as Dad gets acquainted with the CEO guy. Even the tiny bathroom is mostly wood, and it gives me the feeling of being encased in a box. I rush us out as quickly as possible, and we rejoin the men in the kitchen area.

"This building functions as a bed and breakfast of sorts during good times," Russell is explaining to Dad and Nick. "Members can vacation here for a week or two, do some hunting or fishing or what have you. The ranch has many recreational activities—swimming, horseshoes, video games for rainy days...." He smiles at April. "Most of the rooms upstairs are occupied at present, but I think this is where we'll put you, Nick." He nods at Nick, then turns to smile at my father. "And there's a vacant log house for you and your girls, Gabe. All of our log homes have fortified basement rooms, which will serve as shelters in the event of a collapse. Eventually, all the basements will be connected by tunnels, and we'll have our very own underground community."

Dad listens, rapt, as Russell speaks. The bunker blueprint in Mom's recipe book seems so dinky compared to an interconnected underground shelter community.

Two weeks seems impossibly unrealistic. I might never get Dad away from this place.

Everyone else arrives within the hour. After a second flurry of welcomes and introductions, Dennis arranges a late dinner for us—leftover pasta made by a member—and then Russell steps in to show us the grounds.

It's almost dark by this time, and April is growing increasingly tired and cranky. So am I, for that matter. I wrap my fingers securely around hers as Russell jabbers on about the ranch's many virtues.

"As you may have noticed, we like to build using logs," he says as we walk past the lodge. "Not only are they insulating, they also protect against bullets."

Bullets. The word lands hard in my gut, reminding me that as quaint as this place looks, it's not just a remote farm-like setup. I glance at April. Luckily she's focused on watching Max the dog, who's marching alongside Nick ahead of us, seemingly thrilled to be near all these trees and wildlife.

Dane is walking with his parents to the left of us, his hands stuffed into his pockets and his eyes on the shadowy forest. I haven't had a chance to speak to him since we got here, so I have no idea how he feels bring surrounded by all this wood.

Russell pauses near one of the log houses and turns around. "As I mentioned to some of you earlier, we're working on joining the basement rooms of the log homes using underground tunnels. These will connect to our new main shelter, which we're still in the process of building. You can kind of see part of it in the distance there," he adds, pointing. "The structure with the corrugated metal roof."

We all look, and sure enough, there's a large, curved sheet of ridged metal, sticking up out of the ground next to several mounds of dirt and a yellow backhoe. Is that what Dad will be working on? It doesn't exactly look impressive.

"That particular shelter will have radiation detectors and a submarine exit leading to the outside," Russell goes on. "During a crisis period, we'd have guards stationed outside twenty-four-seven. Oh, that reminds me...."

He starts walking again, leading us closer to the woods. April tightens her grip on my hand, eyes wide as she looks up at the quickly darkening sky. I can't blame her—I don't want to be anywhere near these woods in the dark either.

Russell stops and points to something above us. We look up at yet another wooden building, like a treehouse, nestled in the branches of one of the bigger trees. A sturdy-looking ladder runs from the ground to the base of the structure. April's apprehension dissolves as she gapes, her eyes following the length of the ladder like she's wondering how to climb it.

"It looks like a cool treehouse," Russell says with a wink in April's direction. "But it's actually an elevated guard post that looks out over the entire property. Did you notice our beautiful gazebo near the lodge? That's a guard post too."

"Can anyone act as a guard?" Nick asks. His tone is casual, but I can hear the eagerness underneath. Does he like the idea of protecting the place, or does he just want to stand around with a gun? My stomach clenches at the thought of him with a loaded weapon.

"During a collapse, we rely on our membership for manpower," Russell says as we continue walking, our footsteps quiet on the grass. "Everyone takes part in the daily operation of the ranch, whether it be guarding, hunting, or collecting firewood. We're a functioning community."

Nick nods and tosses another glance at the guard tower, like he's picturing himself up there, rifle in hand. I'm starting to wonder if he *wants* an apocalypse, just so he can feel important.

"You folks must be tired," Russell says, checking his watch. "Get some rest, and I'll show you the rest of the property tomorrow afternoon, before your orientation."

Orientation? I'm too tired to worry about what that will involve.

Russell turns to face us again, his mouth curved into a smile. If he were someone else, and we were somewhere else, I might actually like this guy. He has an easy, earnest charm about him. "I'm so pleased to have you all here. Welcome to our ranch."

Russell and Nick head back to the lodge with Max trotting at their heels, leaving Dennis to show the rest of us to our cabins. All the log houses look the same, though a couple are larger than the others and have attached garages. Each family has been assigned to one of the smaller ones, which look to be about half the size of our house. Not that it matters. At this point, I'd sleep in one of the guard posts.

"Isn't this great?" Dad enthuses as we enter our temporary home and flick on the light.

Just as the website pictures promised, the décor is sparse and rustic, and like the rest of the place, it's ninety-nine per cent wood. To the right is a small kitchen area, with basic appliances and a rectangular oak table for four. The living room, which consists of a blue and yellow plaid couch and matching chair, takes up the other side of the space. It looks like any summer cabin, free from electronics and the luxuries of normal life.

"Tomorrow we'll go to the store and stock the kitchen with food," Dad says, sliding our luggage across the smooth wood floor.

April whirls around the room, opening and closing cabinets and testing out the furniture. I stay where I am, frozen by the door, too overwhelmed and exhausted to do anything else. We're finally here, at a survivalist compound in the middle of the wilderness, standing in a cabin made from bulletproof logs.

Dad notices my dazed expression. "Okay, girls, I think we all need a good night's sleep."

For once, I agree. We lug our bags down a short hallway to the bedrooms. There are two—one for Dad and another for April and me to share.

April squeals when we open the door to our room. I almost groan but catch myself. More than half of the cramped space is taken up by a homemade wooden bunk bed, with a double-sized mattress on the bottom and a single on the top. April immediately scales the ladder and sets her crocodile and Twilight Sparkle on the pillow, staking claim to the top bunk. So not only do I have to share a room with my little sister while we're here, I also have to worry about her crashing down on top of me while I sleep.

"Isn't this great?" my father repeats. This time he looks directly at me as he says it, like he's begging for me to agree, to validate his decision to bring us here. To accept it.

Averting my eyes from his, I drop my suitcase on the bed and brush past him to the bathroom, shutting the heavy oak door behind me.

Chapter Fifteen

This place is too quiet, every crack and creak like a gunshot to my ears. It took me hours to get to sleep last night. And when I finally did, I was jolted awake shortly after to find April next to me, curled up on her side with her crocodile clutched in her arms. Even with her night-light plugged in beside the bed, the room was still much darker than we're both used to, so I didn't mind having her there.

The next time I wake up, I'm disoriented and covered in sweat. Sleeping in a room with only the open window for ventilation will take some getting used to. Eyes still shut, I slide one hand across the scratchy sheets, feeling for an April-sized lump. My searching hand meets an empty space on the bed, and I can hear voices coming from another part of the cabin.

"Hold on a sec, Sunshine," I hear my father say, followed by the rustle of a paper bag. "Help me put this stuff away first."

There's a pause, then my sister's voice. "When can we go up in the treehouse?"

"It's not a treehouse. It's a guard tower, and only adults can go up there. It's too dangerous for kids." A cabinet door closes with a bang. "I have some things to do this morning, but maybe your sister can take you to the stables to see the horses after she eats breakfast."

"Yay!"

I sit up, plucking my damp shirt from my skin as I reach for my phone. It's 9:43; I slept in.

I take a shower, then put on shorts and a tank top. When I emerge from the bathroom, my sister and father are no longer in the kitchen. Dad must have gotten up early and gone to the store; a loaf of bread sits on the counter, and shelves of food greet me when I open the fridge. I'm about to pour a bowl of cereal when I hear Dad and April's voices again, this time from below me. Confused, I turn around and face the living room just as a square of wood floor lifts up, revealing April's curly head.

"Izzie!" she says. "There's a secret basement. Come see!"

The hatch in the floor between the kitchen and the living room is about the size of half a door. I hadn't noticed it last night. Peering into it, I see a wooden ladder, its wide slats descending to the concrete ground below. April climbs down again, and cautiously I follow her, gripping the ladder tight as I lower myself into the room.

It's cooler down here, but only slightly. A single hanging bulb illuminates the cramped space, which consists of four platform beds bolted to the plywood walls, shelves packed with canned goods and supplies, a black futon sofa, and a small wooden dining set. There are no windows, or anything to give the illusion that we're still in a house, the outside world just beyond the walls.

My father is examining the contents of the shelves with an expression of deep satisfaction. He finally has his underground bunker.

"Good morning," he says when he finally notices me. "This place is really something, isn't it?"

It's really something, all right. At least he didn't say *Isn't this great?* like he has for everything else. Because there's nothing great about being in here, underground and confined, surrounded by plywood walls that feel like they're slowly closing in around us.

My throat tightens, making it hard to swallow. Or breathe. April and Dad, oblivious, continue to look around, while I stay by the ladder, frozen, convinced that there can't be enough air for one person down here, let alone three.

Unable to speak, I turn and climb back up the ladder, moving much faster than when I climbed down. The smothering feeling eases as I pop back out onto the main floor, but the dark wood is still heavy around me. Desperate for air and open space, I throw open the cabin door and step outside, almost colliding with someone on the porch steps. It's Dane, dressed in a T-shirt and board shorts and carrying a glass container with a red cover.

"Whoa." He jumps aside, almost dropping the container. "Where's the fire?"

In my throat, I think, but I don't say it out loud. "Sorry," I say instead. "I was just...I needed some air."

"Are you okay?" His dark eyes scan my face, which I'm sure is paler than usual.

"Yeah." It's true, I think. The sun feels good on my skin, and my breaths are coming easier now. "What's that?"

He follows my gaze to the glass container in his hands. "Oh, it's this tofu breakfast scramble my mom made. She thought you guys would like some."

"We—I'm not hungry," I say, which is probably rude, but my brain is still muddled from being in the basement shelter. "But thanks," I tack on, because it *is* a nice gesture. On his mom's part.

He smiles, clearly not offended. "I guess I'll eat it, then. Got a fork?"

"Not on me."

This makes him laugh. The sound of it pushes away the lingering prickle of tension in my body, and a nice floaty feeling takes its place.

April bursts outside then, a giant smile on her face. "Daddy said you can take me to see the horses," she says, hopping in place. The boards of the porch shake beneath us.

"Okay," I say before she destroys the place. I glance at Dane, a silent invitation.

"I wouldn't mind getting a look at the horses too," he tells April, who grins even wider. "Just let me unload this breakfast scramble first."

Instead of taking the container back to his cabin, he drops it off with Kendra and James, who are more than happy to receive a hot breakfast, even if it is vegan. The three of us walk across the gravel path toward the opposite end of the ranch, where the actual farmland is. We pass a sprawling field, where three women are picking big ripe strawberries and dropping them into plastic containers. They look at us with either curiosity or suspicion, like they're not used to seeing people under the age of twenty.

As we approach the farm area, three chickens cross in front of us, periodically pausing to peck at the ground. April watches them for a moment, fascinated. "Here, chickie chickie," she says, beckoning to them like they're cats. I wonder if she's made the connection between these birds and the chicken nuggets she loves so much. I'm not about to burst her bubble.

"Hello there!"

A small woman walks toward us, a silver bucket dangling off her hand. It's Roberta, Dennis's wife. In jeans and rubber boots, her dark hair in a messy ponytail, she's a sharp contrast to the impeccably groomed lady I'd seen at that first meeting. Then I remember the overheard conversation between my dad and Dennis and how Dennis referred to Roberta as a "farmer's daughter." Clearly, she knows her way around a place like this.

"Gabe's girls," she says, looking at April and me. Then her gaze flicks to Dane. "And the handsome Hawaiian."

"Only on my mom's side," Dane corrects her with a smile. "I wasn't born there."

Roberta waves a hand, dismissing this. "Are you three here to milk the goats?"

April makes a face. "We came to see the horses."

"Oh, in that case...." She scatters the contents of the bucket—which turns out to be chicken feed—on the dirt behind her. The three chickens come sprinting over, along with several others. "I think Jodi and Misty are still in the corral. Come on, I'll take you back there."

I assume Jodi and Misty are the horses, so I'm surprised when we circle the giant barn and find only one horse, a brown one with a white patch between its eyes, ambling around a rectangular pen. A tall woman in rubber boots like Roberta's walks ahead, her hand gripping a rope that's attached to the horse's harness.

Roberta walks up to the wooden fence. "Hey, Jodi," she calls. "Little girl here wants to say hello to Misty."

Okay, so Jodi is a woman, not a horse. She—Jodi—looks over at us and smiles, then urges the horse—Misty—in our direction. April dashes ahead to join Roberta at the fence, her eyes never leaving the approaching horse.

"What's your name?" Jodi asks my sister as I step up behind her, vaguely anxious about the temperament of this giant animal. I don't think I've ever been this close to a horse before.

"April." She gazes up at Misty, her eyes like saucers.

"That's a pretty name. I'm Jodi and this is my favorite horse, Misty. She's a big ol' sweetheart."

Roberta introduces Dane and me, and Jodi turns her bright smile on us. She looks to be around my dad's age, maybe a couple years younger, and she's really pretty up close, with wide blue eyes and shiny brown hair reaching halfway down her back.

"You all must be new here," she says, running a hand over the horse's neck. "I don't think I've seen you around."

"We just got here last night," Dane says.

April, bored with the conversation, inches closer to the horse. "Can I pet her?" she asks Jodi.

"Of course!" Jodi says. "She's very friendly."

She tries to gently guide the horse's head lower so April can reach, but Misty isn't having it. Seeing this, Dane catches my eye. "I can..." he says, gesturing to April. When I nod, he lowers his arms toward her, silently offering her a boost. She immediately lifts her own arms in response, and he scoops her up easily, angling her toward Misty's face.

"Can I ride her?" April asks, one arm looped around Dane's neck as she pets the horse's forehead. Misty doesn't seem to mind.

"Not right now, I'm afraid," Jodi says. "One of our member families reserved all six of our horses for a long trail ride this afternoon, and I need to get them ready. But if you come back and visit us tomorrow, maybe you could take a short ride around the paddock on Misty here. She's the perfect horse for beginners."

April nods, satisfied with this arrangement, and I take it as our cue to leave Jodi to her horse wrangling. Dane sets April down, and she waves wildly at Misty before we head back the way we came.

The second the log homes come into sight, April sprints ahead, leaving Dane and me to walk side by side, alone.

"You and April don't really look alike," Dane says, as if he's been thinking it over.

"She looks like our mom." The second the words are out, I regret them. I don't want to talk about my mom right now, especially with someone I barely know. "She died a couple of years ago," I add before I can stop myself. What is wrong with me?

"I heard," he says. "I'm sorry."

I look at the ground. "Thanks."

Silence stretches between us, long and slightly awkward. I start to think about how cute he looked, holding my sister as she made friends with the horse, and a surge of heat hits my face.

"So, um," I say, pushing through the awkwardness. "Do you go back to Hawaii often?" Then I remember he's not from there, his mother is, and he wouldn't be *going back* if he never lived there in the first place. My brain is still about as scrambled as his mom's tofu breakfast dish.

Luckily, Dane either misses my slip or chooses to ignore it. "I've visited a few times. My grandparents still live there, in Kaneohe."

Our pace slows as we get closer to the cabins. "Does your mom miss it?"

"Sometimes." He rakes his fingers through his hair, smoothing it off his face. His bracelet—the same tan hemp one he always wears—slides down his wrist a bit. "This is her home now, though. She moved to Weldon right after college, for a teaching job, and she fell in love with the snow and cold winters. And with my father too, I guess."

I glance at him sharply. This, I wasn't expecting. "Oh. You mean...."

He shoots me a smile, like he's used to people's surprise. "Yeah, my mom used to date men too. She was with my father for two years. He's a teacher too, or he was back then. I'm not sure what he's doing now. He dumped my mom when she told him she was pregnant with me, and we haven't heard from him since. He didn't want to be a dad."

I wince in sympathy. My father may have issues, but he's always been present. As far as I know, he's happy being our dad. "Is your father Hawaiian too?"

"No, he's white." He kicks a loose rock on the path, sending it flying into the grass. "Also a jackass, apparently."

"Yeah, no kidding."

We're just a few yards away from the log houses now, and I look around for April. Finally, I spot her twirling around on the grass by our cabin, a juice box in hand.

"Anyway," Dane says as our pace slackens even more, "it all worked out. She met my other mom a couple of years later, and they got married when I was four. Then she adopted me and gave me her last name, so...." He shrugs. "Sometimes dads are overrated."

As if on cue, my own dad emerges from our cabin and says something to April that I can't make out from here. She pauses to respond, then continues with her aimless twirling. Dad watches her from the porch for a moment, his smile visible even from here, before disappearing back inside.

"Sometimes," I agree, looking back at Dane. "And sometimes they're just really complicated."

Chapter Sixteen

As promised, Russell appears again later in the afternoon to finish the ranch tour for the new arrivals. This time, he leads us through the various fruit and vegetable crops as he chatters on about the importance of a sustainable food supply during a collapse.

"We don't just stockpile nonperishables here," he says, turning to address us as we walk single file through a patch of raspberry bushes. Dad and April are at the head of the pack with Kendra and James behind them, baby Micah strapped to James's back. Nick and his dog are in the middle, while I bring up the rear behind Dane and his parents. "The food we get from hunting and fishing and these gardens—plus our stores of beans and canned goods—would be enough to feed all our members for at least a year."

Charlene raises her hand. "I have a lot of experience in canning."

"Excellent," Russell says, nodding approvingly. "Basic survival skills have all but disappeared in the modern age, but they still come in handy around here."

As we emerge from the bushes, I spot April stuffing a huge handful of raspberries in her mouth as she skips along beside our father. Dane notices too and glances back at me with an amused smirk. I'd laugh if I wasn't so disoriented by the sweeping vastness of this place.

We walk past the currently empty barn and corral and keep going to the livestock area, which seems to consist of several free-range chickens and a couple of goats in a fenced-off shed.

"We don't currently raise cattle here," Russell says, pausing to face us again. "We get most of our meat from a nearby farm, but we're hoping to invest in a heifer or two in the next year or so."

A disapproving look passes between Charlene and Kiana, the resident vegans of our group. Russell, oblivious, continues toward the chicken coops. As we approach, Max suddenly starts barking and straining against his leash. A few seconds later, a big black and white dog lopes toward Russell and almost knocks him over. He rights himself, laughing, and leans down to pet its shaggy coat.

"This is our guard dog, Juno," he says, looping his fingers through the dog's collar. "She protects the chickens from foxes and coyotes and other critters."

Nick keeps a tight hold on Max's leash as he inches closer to Juno. I assumed an animal raised by someone like Nick would be quick-tempered and ready to attack, but all Max does is sniff the other dog and spin around with a plaintive whine, like he just wants to play. April lets out a loud sneeze, her allergies no match for two dogs.

"Let's move on," Russell says. "I have one more place to show you."

He leads us past the farmland to the very edge of the property, where the forest opens up to a narrow dirt road just big enough for one vehicle. We walk down it, not talking, our feet kicking up dust in the dry afternoon heat. Finally, after about twenty minutes or so, the forest opens up again into a huge grassy field. On one side, about a dozen wooden stands are spread out along the tree line, each one with a paper silhouette of a person's head and torso attached to the front. Sweat drips down my back as I stare at the target—a small white *x* directly over the spot where the heart would be.

"This, as you can see, is our shooting range," Russell says, hands on his hips as he surveys the field. "We offer defensive firearm training to all our members."

I think of the pictures on the website—people aiming guns at imaginary threats, preparing themselves for a day when they might need to confront the real thing. A shiver runs through me despite the heat.

"But it's not mandatory, right?" Kendra asks. She's holding the baby now, patting his back as he dozes against her shoulder.

"Well, no, but it's certainly recommended. Anyone over ten years old and licensed can learn to shoot. *Should* learn, in my humble opinion." He smiles, his gaze sweeping over the rest of us. "'By failing to prepare, you are preparing to fail.'"

Nick nods in agreement, eyes locked on the human-shaped targets in the distance like he's imagining shredding them all with holes. Out of the corner of my eye, I see Kiana toss Charlene another troubled glance as she threads an arm through Dane's, nudging him closer. Even April is quiet, her hand clutching Dad's as they both peer out at the range, her with curiosity and him with a pensive expression I can't quite read.

"We should probably head back now," Russell says cheerfully. "It's almost time for orientation."

Ranch orientation for newcomers takes place at the lodge in what Russell calls the "community room"—a small, stuffy space off the dining area with three rows of folding chairs, a big rotating fan, and a flat-screen TV on the wall. When we enter, Dennis and a stocky man in a baseball cap are already standing at the head of the room, along with—surprisingly—Jodi, the woman from the horse corral. I take a seat in the back with April and Dad, relieved to be out of the sun for a while.

"Have a seat, folks," Russell says in his breezy drawl. "I'd like to introduce you to some of our wonderful staff."

I peek over at Dane as he sits up front with his moms and wonder if he's feeling as overwhelmed with this place as I am. He doesn't seem to be; I caught him yawning twice on the tour, and now he's slouching in his chair like he's about to suffer through a boring lecture in class.

"As you know," Russell says as he joins the others at the front of the room, "I'm Colonel Russell Pruitt, CEO and manager here at Endurance Ranch. And you all know Dennis Iverson, our assistant ranch manager."

Dennis smiles and bows his head. Assistant manager? No one else in the room seems surprised about this former military prepper guy securing a leadership role already.

"The gentleman in the blue cap is Bryan Oakley, our construction manager." Russell beams at his audience. "We have Mr. Oakley to thank for our log buildings and underground shelters, including the amazing five-thousand-square-foot shelter that's currently being built."

My father sits up straighter. This is his territory.

"And lastly, we have Jodi Akins, office manager and head of sales. Not only does Ms. Akins deal with memberships, but she's also quite the skilled equestrian."

Jodi smiles and gives a little wave. April waves back, excited to see the horse lady again. Jodi has traded her barn clothes for a tank top and denim shorts that show off her long legs, a detail not missed by Nick in the front row.

"Now I want to speak a little about the objective and function of Endurance Ranch," Russell says, standing with his hands clasped behind his back. "What we're doing here is fulfilling an unmet need. In a collapse, economic activity ceases. Daily food shipments stop, and people start getting hungry. They turn to theft and violence. There's a widespread loss of law and order, high fatalities. Will the government save us? No. They'll prioritize top leadership officials and leave the rest of us to fend for ourselves. And that's what we're aiming to do here—secure the survival of ourselves and our families."

For the first time today, Charlene and Kiana both nod in agreement with Russell. When I glance over to gauge Dad's reaction, he's listening with the same expression he had last night when Russell mentioned the underground tunnels. It's unsettling how captivated he already seems with this place.

"We're programmed by nature to ignore the unlikely," Russell continues. He starts to pace back and forth, hands still fastened behind him. "But you all know as well as I do that our economy is more vulnerable and unstable than ever before. The risk of bioterrorism and nuclear war is rising rapidly due to new technologies. It's easier than ever for a terrorist group or even an individual to create a highly lethal virus that could potentially wipe out most of the population. And that's just one example. Many events could trigger a collapse that lasts for years, and most people aren't equipped to handle that."

I squirm in my seat, glad that April's distracted peeling the banana she got from the kitchen on the way in and doesn't seem to be listening.

Dennis nods solemnly at Russell. "Home basements and backyard bunkers won't cut it when the shit hits the fan, folks," he says in his booming voice. "You need room to spread out, to quarantine against illness. You need several guards who work in shifts to protect the property. Unless you have the expertise and equipment required to fight and survive, your best bet is to join a large, organized community that works together and shares expenses. If you present a strong, fortified compound, marauders will look elsewhere."

"Damn right," Nick says loudly.

Russell's eyes narrow slightly at the interruption, but he shakes it off. "We can't predict the likelihood of disaster, but we can prepare for the impact. And that's what this community is all about."

He stops pacing and unclasps his hands, holding them out like he's making an offering. Which I suppose he is. This entire orientation has been like a sales pitch for lifelong protection against every threat imaginable. As if any of that is guaranteed.

"Now," Russell continues, his tone lightening. "I'm going to give the floor to Ms. Akins, who has a few things to say about our membership options."

Jodi smooths her long hair over one shoulder and steps forward. "Hi, everyone. Welcome."

Baby Micah, who's been quietly lounging on his father's lap since we sat down, suddenly lets out a squawk. Jodi flashes a smile at him before launching into her portion of the pitch.

"Survivalist communities like Endurance Ranch are an

affordable way to survive a long-term disaster situation. In a declared emergency, members have access to our supplies and underground shelters. But in good times—like now—the ranch functions as an outdoor recreation facility. This membership model works because not only do you get a secure place to ride out a collapse, but you also get a vacation spot you can visit anytime you want." She smiles again. "Of course, all members are expected to contribute to the property's upkeep."

Kendra raises a hand. "If the economy did collapse, I assume the demand for membership would surge beyond the ranch's capacity. How is it decided who gets in and who doesn't?"

"Members have priority when there's a wait list," Jodi assures her. "Now, the upfront fee is the same for everyone, but quarterly membership dues depend on the size of accommodation you need. The rooms in the new shelter will have the capacity to house anyone from a single person right up to a six-person family."

"Sorry, I have a question as well," James says, handing the whimpering baby to his wife. "Are members vetted? I mean, Kendra and I work in IT and even we had to go through criminal record checks before joining our companies. You spoke about how economic collapse would trigger a loss of law and order, but how would law and order be maintained in here?"

Russell steps forward. "All excellent questions," he says smoothly. "Our members help keep this place running, but Endurance Ranch is always under the control of Dennis and myself. We're both former military. I also have a degree in security management. Trust me...even if law and order fails out there, we're both highly qualified to enforce it in here."

The room grows quiet for a moment. Even Micah stops

fussing. In the silence, I try to imagine what life would look like here after a collapse. Armed guards everywhere. Rationing food and water and medications. Possibly quarantining underground for weeks or months or forever, never knowing what horror waits outside. Always worried about poisoned air or some fatal virus breaching the walls and killing you and everyone you love. Spending the rest of your days fenced in and fighting to survive. Alive, but not thriving.

They're already living half in this disaster zone, and it hasn't even happened yet.

"Izzie." April taps my arm with her slimy banana fingers. "I'm thirsty."

I stand up and take her hand, glad for an excuse to get out of here. We've been here for less than twenty-four hours, and all I want to do is escape.

Chapter Seventeen

"Jodi says I'm a natural."

April says the last word slowly, like it doesn't fit in her six-year-old-sized mouth. I force myself not to roll my eyes. Since our first visit to the corral, it's been *Jodi says* and *Jodi this* and *Jodi that*. It bothers me. Maybe because April hasn't mentioned Mom even once since we got here.

"I'm not surprised," Dad says, smiling at her in the rearview mirror. "Yesterday she told me she's never seen someone so young take to riding so quickly."

April grins back at him, pleased. We haven't seen our father for two days—since the orientation, he's been spending most of his time at the new shelter construction— but he showed up at the cabin this afternoon, sweaty and dirty, and asked if we wanted to go into town with him to pick up a vernier caliper, whatever that is. I jumped at the chance to get off the ranch for a little while, even though the "town" is just a strip of road about twenty minutes down the highway that mainly consists of a grocery store, a hardware store, a post office, and a restaurant that operates out of an old silver trailer. Not exactly a metropolis.

Dad and April slipped right into the rhythm of the ranch, but after three full days here, I'm still adjusting to the surroundings. The acres of woods and fields are too quiet, the wooden walls of the buildings monotonous and, at worst, suffocating. There's only so much exploring April and I can do before she gets bored and insists we head to the corral to see if Jodi and Misty are around. When they are, April gets to ride for a half hour or so closely monitored by Jodi. It's the highlight of her day.

My only highlight is my occasional run-in with Dane, who seems to spend a lot of time in the woods, hiking and looking for edible plants. So far, we've talked about little more than the plants or berries he's found, though I've refused to eat any of them. The bitter taste of the backyard chickweed is still fresh in my mind. Still, his cheerful, laid-back presence is about the only thing I look forward to here.

The town's hardware store is about the size of one of our convenience stores back home, but it appears to have all the basics. Dad goes off in search for his caliper or whatever, and April follows, excited for somewhere new to explore. I hang back and slowly peruse the nuts-and-bolts section, grateful for a few minutes of solitude.

"Need a hand finding something, honey?"

I turn to see a gray-haired woman with glasses standing a few feet away. She's wearing a green apron and holding a cardboard box under one arm.

"Oh. No, thanks." I drop the small silver washer I was holding back into its cubby. "I'm just waiting for my dad."

She smiles and starts transferring the items in the box into another cubby. Screwnails, it looks like. "You and your dad just passing through? We don't see many new faces around here."

She's clearly just being polite—and maybe a touch nosey too—but I don't mind. It's a nice change to talk to someone who isn't about to slip into a tirade about nuclear war and bioterrorism any second.

"No," I say, picking up a box of roofing nails. "We're visiting the survival community near Westlake Forest. Endurance Ranch."

"How nice," the woman says, smiling at me again as she finishes restocking the screwnails.

I'm not sure if she actually heard me or if ranch discussion is common enough around here to be boring. In any case, our chitchat ends there, and the woman nods at me before disappearing from the aisle. I replace the box of nails. Dad must have found his caliper thing by now.

As I'm passing the next aisle, a hand closes around my forearm, making me jump. I look up, expecting to see my father, but it's Nick.

"What are you doing?" he asks me through clenched teeth. His pale face is flushed, not in patches this time but a solid mass of red.

I'm so surprised that I can't answer for a moment. "Shopping," I finally say. I try to pull my arm out of his grip, but he holds on. "Let go of me."

He ignores me. "You were talking to that woman about the ranch."

He must have overheard us as he shopped for his— whatever is in the stack of green and yellow boxes in his other hand. I yank my arm again, and this time he lets go. My skin feels damp where he gripped it. "So?"

He stares at me for a moment. His eyes, I notice for the first time, are light blue. Cold. "*So*, you're not supposed to talk about it to people you don't know. It's not a public place where just anyone can drop in. Only members and trusted friends of members know the precise location."

I glance around for Dad and April, but all I see is another green-aproned employee, straightening a display of lightbulbs. "It was just some random woman."

He transfers the boxes to his other hand, and I catch a glimpse of the label on the top one. *Rifle cartridges.* He's buying *bullets*. I know Nick probably spends the majority of his time at the shooting range, but why is he buying his own bullets? Is the stockpile at the ranch not enough for him?

Nick crosses his arms over his T-shirt, which I just now notice has the jaguar logo. "What happens if the shit hits the fan and that random woman tells the entire town about the nearby survival ranch near the forest?" He leans his face into mine, his musty breath fanning across my cheeks. "You think they're not all going to rush over there, expecting to just waltz in past the guards? There would be anarchy."

Prickly heat floods my face; my skin is probably as red as his. Nothing about this trip has been fun, but getting scolded in the middle of a hardware store by some jerk I barely know has got to be the lowest of the low.

"If you can't keep the ranch a secret," Nick says, leaning in even more so I'll hear every word, "then maybe you shouldn't be part of it."

With that, he walks away, boxes of bullets clutched in his hands. I glance around again, but it's still just me, standing alone in the quiet aisle, heartbeat loud in my ears.

"I don't want to be part of it," I mumble, even though he's long gone.

"I saw Nick at the hardware store," I tell my father on the way back to the ranch.

"Oh?" He's distracted by a pickup truck on our tail, getting ready to pass us on the narrow highway.

"He overheard me mentioning the ranch to an employee and he got mad."

Dad slows to let the truck pass, then glances at me. "Why were you talking about the ranch with someone at the store?"

"It was just a comment. But Nick—"

"Nick is a hothead, Isobel," he says, eyes on the road ahead. "Don't pay any attention to him."

My skin tingles where his sweaty fingers were clamped a few minutes ago. "But he—"

"Daddy, can I play in the secret basement room when we get home?" April cuts in from the back seat.

"Sure, Sunshine."

I can't decide which disturbs me more—Nick, Dad's brush-off, or April calling the ranch "home" and wanting to play underground.

By the time we get back to the ranch, hot anger is still churning around inside me, and I feel like I might burst if I don't release it somehow. Since my father clearly doesn't care, there's only one other person here I can think of who might listen.

"Hey," Dane says when he opens his cabin door to my knock. "Change your mind about trying the huckleberries?"

Relief cuts through some of the anger. I'm so glad he's here and not wandering around in the woods somewhere. "Want to take a walk?"

Something in my voice, or on my face, makes him pause for a second, his smile drooping. "Sure," he says, stepping outside.

We head for the open, grassy field behind the log homes and walk slowly around the perimeter as I spill it all out. The innocent chat with the woman in the hardware store, Nick's reproach, my humiliation, Dad's apathy about what happened. Dane stays silent through the entire thing, just listening.

"I don't like the guy," I finish, my anger almost spent. "He's a jerk, and he scares me. He's *too* into this lifestyle, you know? It's like...he was this outcast who finally found somewhere to belong, and now he's on a huge power trip."

"Nick is kind of an asshole," Dane says in a careful tone. "There's no doubt about that."

The sun is bright and shining directly on us, but I can still make out the torn expression on his face.

"But..." I prompt because there's clearly one coming.

"What he said is true," he says, wincing a bit. "I mean, the way he said it was wrong, ambushing you like that in the store and being such a dick about it. But there's a reason this place doesn't advertise where it is. It's a big property, sure, but there's still only so much room and supplies to go around." He glances behind us, toward the lodge, its big windows sparkling in the sun. "That's why our parents all signed that contract."

"What contract?"

"Oh, right, you and April left the meeting early the other day." He kicks at a weed in the grass. "After the orientation was over, they all signed some kind of non-disclosure agreement thing. Everyone over eighteen who visits here has to promise they'll keep the place a secret."

Why didn't Dad tell me about this? Not knowing makes me feel even more alone, like everyone else is playing a game and I'm standing on the sidelines, unsure of the rules.

"Well, *I* didn't sign anything," I say, folding my arms. I don't care about orders from ranch management. "So that means I'm free to tell anyone I want, right?"

"Yeah, technically, but just by being here we're agreeing to follow their rules. It's sort of understood."

"Not by me." I stop walking and turn to face him, squinting against the sunlight. "How can you be so...*unaffected* by all this? You seem almost bored when everyone talks about the world imploding and you don't seem to mind that your parents just picked up and moved you here. Aren't you homesick?"

He shrugs one shoulder. "All the stuff Russell and the preparedness group says...none of that is new to me. And yeah, I get homesick, but that's not new to me either. My moms like to move around a lot. When I was little, we lived on a houseboat for two years, so a survivalist ranch doesn't seem all that strange to me, you know?"

"It does to me. I never agreed to come here."

The anger starts building again, intensified by exhaustion and fear and the utter surreal-ness of being here, but instead of storming off or screaming at Dane, I burst into tears.

"Isobel?"

I register Dane's voice, soft and concerned, and then his hand, featherlight on my arm. Without any thought or hesitation, I lean into him, my forehead resting in the hollow between his shoulder and neck. "I miss my mom," I whisper into his shirt.

Slowly, his arms come around me, and we stand there together for a while, embracing on the sunburned grass.

Chapter Eighteen

Russell invites us to join him at the main lodge for breakfast on Saturday. I'm surprised he only comes around for potential-member orientations and weekends and doesn't live on the property in one of the larger log homes at the edge of the forest. I don't want to have breakfast with him, but April is adamant about eating pancakes and I don't want her in a room full of prepper bigwigs alone.

Apparently, we're not the only ones who got the invite. When we enter the lodge dining room, Nick is talking animatedly to Russell. Dane and his parents are here too, along with Jodi, the horse lady, and a handful of people I vaguely recognize. The only ones missing from our group are James, Kendra, and baby Micah.

"They left early this morning," Dad says with a frown when I comment on their absence. "Decided the ranch wasn't for them."

I feel a pang of sadness. I never got to know them well, but they definitely seemed like two of the more level-headed members of the group.

Russell eases himself away from Nick and invites us all to sit. I settle in between my father and sister and survey the spread in front of us. The long dining table is loaded with food—different kinds of meat, eggs cooked various ways, platters piled high with fruit and toast and pancakes. My stomach growls despite my nervousness at sharing a table with Nick and Dane, each for different reasons. Nick hasn't even glanced at me, but I can feel Dane's eyes on me across the table. I'm not sure why I feel embarrassed every time I look at him now. He's been nothing but kind to me since I wept all over him the other day.

"Good morning, everyone," Russell says, taking a seat at the head of the table. "I want to thank you all for joining me this morning. Please, help yourselves to this feast Sonya and Penny have cooked up for us."

April immediately spears a pancake and drops it onto her plate. Everyone else follows her lead, passing dishes down the table. I scoop up some scrambled eggs, half-listening to Nick as he continues his mostly one-sided conversation with Russell.

"...no disrespect, Colonel, but I don't think your generation has fully grasped the advancements in biotechnology. The world is more vulnerable to DNA manipulation than ever. Not to mention artificial intelligence is a risk to the entire existence of human civilization."

Russell cuts into a sausage and chuckles. "Oh, I'm aware, Nick." He pops the piece into his mouth and turns to my father. "Gabe," he says, leaning toward him. "The progress on the new shelter is impressive. Dennis was right when he said you'd fit in beautifully here."

My father grins modestly while Nick saws into his pancake like it's a piece of overcooked meat. "It's a great crew. Thanks for having us. We're really enjoying the ranch."

Russell smiles at April and me. "Glad to hear it."

April, genial as always, grins back at him, while I stuff a piece of bacon into my mouth. My gaze skims over Dane again and lands directly on Jodi, who's watching my father in a way I don't like. Like she's trying to hide the fact that she's looking at him. Exactly the way I'm probably looking at Dane.

The bacon in my mouth suddenly turns into a tasteless, chewy glob. I press my napkin to my mouth and discreetly spit it out.

As if sensing my eyes on her, Jodi stops goggling at my father and turns to me. "Oh, what a beautiful bracelet!"

I follow her gaze to my wrist, where my mother's sterling silver bracelet is glinting in the sunlight streaming through the windows. "Thanks," I mumble, moving my arm out of view.

It didn't take me long to fix the bracelet. I did it the night before we left, while Dad and April were asleep. A new toggle clasp and a little polish, and it's as good as new. I don't know why I decided to put it on this morning. Maybe I need a little piece of Mom with me, something I can look at and touch whenever I want. I know she wouldn't have minded me wearing it.

Dad, on the other hand? Going by the unsettled look on his face, I'm not so sure.

"Where did you find that bracelet?" he asks quietly.

"It was in Mom's car," I tell him, taking a gulp of orange juice.

April leans toward me. "What's it say on the heart?"

I show her the pewter charm and she sounds out the word, smiling when she gets it.

"Always," Dad repeats with a short, bitter laugh.

My appetite is now gone, so I push my food around my plate for the rest of breakfast. After, everyone jumps up to help clear the dishes. Except for me, because I'm too busy watching Jodi sidle up to my father, smiling as she reaches in front of him to grab a casserole dish. He gives her a quick smile back and continues stacking empty plates.

I sit there, frozen and fuming. How dare she flirt with my father like that? And how dare he smile back at her like he's enjoying her attention?

Well, I refuse to stay here and watch. I get up and slip outside, pausing near a tall, carved statue of a bear standing guard at the front of the lodge. Inhaling deeply, I try to calm the hot anger churning in my stomach.

The door opens behind me. "Hey," Dane says when he spots me. He walks toward me, car keys dangling from his hand. "What's wrong?"

Tears sting my eyes but I blink them away, refusing to cry in front of him for a second time. "Nothing. I'm fine."

He peers at me, unsure. "I'm just heading into town. Do you want to come along?"

I hesitate for a moment. Dad's heading to the construction site soon and I'm supposed to watch April, like I do every day. Then an image of him and Jodi, standing together and laughing, flashes through my mind. Screw it. If I have to be stuck here, I refuse to spend every waking minute watching April so my father can go build a bulletproof bunker for Colonel Russell.

"Let's go," I say.

It's a quiet ride into town—I guess things *are* a little awkward between us. Dane fiddles with the stereo while I examine the interior of the car. It's neat and smells vaguely minty, like Dane himself. Something about it relaxes me.

"Just need to pick up a few things for my mom," Dane says as he pulls the car into a space in front of the grocery store.

I don't really need anything, but I'm content to tag along beside Dane as he hits up the fruit and vegetables aisle, followed by the small organics section. When we wander into the pharmacy area, he hesitates for a moment before grabbing a stick of deodorant and placing it in the basket next to a bag of quinoa.

"Your mom uses men's deodorant?" I ask, raising my brow at him.

He grins and keeps walking. "It's for me. It's one of my mini battles, I guess. My parents think regular antiperspirant causes cancer because it has aluminum and parabens and all these other chemicals. They want me to use the natural kind, but it just doesn't cut it, you know? So I use the hard stuff in secret."

I laugh. "That explains why you always smell so nice."

He looks at me, his cheeks flushing slightly. Oh God. Did I really just say that out loud? To his face? In my embarrassment, I reach for something on the shelf closest to me, which turns out to be a box of denture cleaner. I pretend to examine it for a second, then put it back. Jesus. I need to change the subject, and fast.

"So, if that's a mini battle, what's the big battle?" I ask as we turn into the next aisle—cookies and snacks.

He pauses before saying, "Measles."

I turn. "Huh?"

"I told you my parents don't trust the government, right? Well, they don't trust the World Health Organization either." He picks up a box of chocolate chip cookies then immediately puts it back on the shelf. "They never had me vaccinated."

I stare at him. "Oh my God."

"Yeah. And now that all these old childhood illnesses are making a comeback...." He sighs. "I've spent a lot of time researching, and the stuff I've learned totally contradicts what my parents have always said about vaccines basically poisoning people."

I think about the first time I saw him, in the medical section of the library. "But vaccines save lives. They help more than they hurt."

"I know. That's why I want to get vaccinated as soon as possible."

"Can't you just go to the doctor and get it done?"

"Not without my parents' consent, and they'll never give it. I've asked," he adds before I can ask. "I have to wait until I'm eighteen, which isn't until February."

I nod, thinking how unfair it is that we're both basically powerless until we hit that magic number. Legally unable to detach ourselves from the situations our parents put us in, supposedly for our own protection. But in whose eyes?

"So, do you actually believe in all this?"

"What? That vaccines and regular deodorant poison people? I don't think—"

"No." Realizing how vague I sounded, I try again. "I mean doomsday. TEOTWAWKI." The acronym rolls easily off my tongue now. "Do you think it's imminent, like everyone at the ranch believes, or do you think the media makes the world seem scarier than it actually is?"

Dane's quiet as he thinks this over. The store is virtually empty this time of day, so the only sounds are our footsteps and the peppy eighties music playing over the intercom.

"I wouldn't say it's *imminent*," he says, pausing in front of the chocolate and candy shelf. "But possible? Sure."

"And does that scare you?"

He locates the peanut butter cups and puts three packages in his basket. "Of course, but there's not much we can do about it besides prepare ourselves for the possibility."

"But super volcanos, electrical grid failure, nuclear attacks..." I count off each atrocity on my fingers. "Do you think the chances of these things happening are so high that we need to rearrange our entire lives around them? Instead of, say, working toward making the world better and having faith that things will turn out okay?"

He shrugs. "I understand both sides. Unlike my parents, I don't see everything as black or white, good or bad. Good definitely outweighs the bad with some things, though."

"Like vaccinations."

"And effective deodorant."

I smile. "Definitely."

We start walking again, this time in the direction of the cash registers. There's more I want to say—it's nice talking about my doubts with someone who doesn't automatically spout off a list of potential disasters to scare me back in line—but I also don't want him to think I'm criticizing him or his life with his parents. Because we're *not* our parents, even when we're stuck on the same path as them.

"I think it's important to be ready," Dane says as he unloads his items onto the conveyor belt. "But it's also important to be hopeful." He stops unloading and nudges my shoulder with his. "See? I told you I can see both sides."

The cashier shoots us an impatient look, but I don't care. I laugh, and everything falls away for a moment—my worry, my homesickness, the ranch, Jodi. It seems impossible that I could experience any fun or lightness in this place, but here in this crappy grocery store with Dane, I can almost forget where we are and why we're here.

"Um, Dane," I say once we're back on the highway. The sunshine from earlier has disappeared behind a layer of gray clouds. "I'm sorry about the other day. The crying, I mean. I was upset, and I needed to vent to someone. This place really gets to me sometimes, and I just—I don't know."

"No need to apologize." A few drops of rain hit the windshield and he turns the wipers on. "This place gets to me sometimes too. Why do you think I spend so much time in the woods?"

I look at him, surprised. He seems like such a go-with-the-flow type, happy to be wherever he finds himself. Like April. It never occurred to me that sometimes he might feel like I do—lonely and overwhelmed and desperate to connect with someone who understands.

My gaze shifts from Dane's face to the long, open road ahead of us. Maybe we could be that someone for each other.

Chapter Nineteen

It's raining hard when we get back to the ranch, so Dane and I head for the lodge to wait it out and check our phones. Wi-Fi in the cabins is virtually nonexistent, but the signal in the main building is strong enough for a few minutes of service.

When we get inside, I'm surprised to see April in the kitchen with Dane's moms, who appear to be making some kind of dessert. Kiana hands April a spoon, and she starts stirring something in a bowl while Kiana measures out brown sugar and Charlene lines a pan with parchment paper. They're clearly having fun, laughing and joking as they move around the big kitchen.

"Izzie!" April waves at me with her free hand. "We're making strawberry crumble."

I smile at her and glance around the lodge, which—just a couple of hours ago—was full of people eating breakfast at the long pine table. Now it's quiet, aside from two couples playing cards at the cleared table and Nick, who's sitting in the living room with his laptop open on his lap and an irritated expression on his face. Max, as usual, is at his feet, stretched out and dozing. Nick doesn't acknowledge my presence, but my muscles still tense like they do every time I'm in his vicinity. I focus on my sister again and try to pretend like he doesn't exist.

"Where's Dad?" I ask.

She shrugs, so I look to Kiana and Charlene.

"He came in a half hour ago and asked us to watch April," Kiana says, playfully swatting Dane's hand as he snatches a strawberry from a bowl on the counter. "He didn't say where he was going."

Just as she says this, the door bangs open and my father appears, his hair and shirt damp from the rain. He pauses when he sees me and shuts his eyes for a moment, letting out a breath. Then he strides over to me, his expression turning darker with each step.

"Where have you *been*?"

The harshness of his tone catches me off guard, and it takes me a second to answer. "I went to the store with Dane."

"The store." He rubs a hand over his face. "I've been looking all over for you, Isobel. I thought you got lost in the woods or something."

I glance at April. She's watching Dad with wide eyes, her spoon frozen mid-stir, while Kiana and Charlene quietly work around her. Dane stares at his phone screen like it's suddenly incredibly interesting.

"You can't just leave without telling me where you're going," Dad continues. "I need you to stay with your sister."

My face burns. "Can we talk about this later?"

"I'm supposed to be working on the shelter right now," Dad goes on like I haven't even spoken. "Instead, I've been running all over the place searching for you."

Behind me, Nick lets out a snicker. "Waste of time."

Everyone, including the people playing cards, turns to look at him. He keeps his eyes on his laptop, a slight smirk on his lips.

"What did you say?" my father asks, his voice taking on a darker, almost threatening tinge.

Nick looks up, unfazed. "Building that big new shelter, I mean. It's a waste of time. We don't need more hiding places around here." He sits up straight, his still-open laptop sliding down his legs. "What we need is a wall."

"A wall," Kiana repeats, eyebrows raised. "What for?"

"If a big group of marauders decides to advance on us through the woods, there won't be enough guards to stop them," he says in that fired-up way he has, eyes dancing with excitement. "If we had, say, a twenty-foot-high concrete wall spanning the entire perimeter, not even a goddamn Olympic pole-vaulter would be able to get over it."

"Twenty feet of concrete?" Dad shakes his head and turns back to me, dismissing Nick's ramblings. From his face, I can tell he's not done embarrassing me in front of everyone.

"It's doable." Nick closes his laptop and stands up. "I read about a survivalist community in Colorado that has one. Makes it easier to get a clean shot from the guard tower when you have their backs against a wall, so to speak."

Charlene leans over the counter, her face scrunched like she just tasted something bad. "Are you actually talking about shoot—" She pauses and glances at April, who's gone back to stirring but is clearly listening. "Uh, taking people out?"

Nick fixes his cold blue gaze on her. "What did you think we'd do to someone who tries to infiltrate the property? Invite them in for strawberry crumble?"

Her lips go thin, and she takes a step back. Dane shoots Nick a glare, which he either doesn't notice or pretends not to.

"A wall of that size would take years to build," Dad tells him. "Not to mention the cost of materials for a structure of that scale."

Nick crosses his arms over his Endurance Ranch T-shirt. "Well, I mentioned it to Dennis and Russell, and they both think it's a good idea."

"It's not that I'm *against* building a defensive wall, Nick," Dad says, now with his full attention. "I'm just saying we need to be practical. This is what I do for a living...I analyze the cost of materials and equipment needed for construction projects. And the kind of project you're talking about would probably end up bankrupting the place. It would make more sense just to wall off a specific area of the ranch rather than the entire property."

Nick's smirk slides back in place. "I appreciate your input, Gabe, but it's not really up to you, is it? Only paying members get a say on big decisions around here, and last I checked, you're the only *visitor* left on the ranch."

The room goes quiet as Dad and Nick scowl at each other. I'm not sure what to feel—relieved that we're *not* members or angry at Nick for being such a raging dick to my father, even though I'm mad at him too. So I just stand there, motionless and mute, as the tension that's been building between them for the past couple of weeks thickens in the air like smoke.

"This is our safety we're talking about," Nick says, stepping closer. "Say a genetically engineered super virus started circulating. You really want to risk strangers bringing that in? If everyone here is as committed to the community as they should be, then they'll gladly pitch in for a defensive wall."

"I'm committed to this place," Dad fires back at him. "If I wasn't, I wouldn't be here busting my ass every day on its expansion."

"Well, part of the expansion should include a wall. It's well worth the time and money to have the extra layer of protection."

"More like an extra layer of isolation," I mutter.

Nick turns his glare on me, redness creeping up his face. "You keep out of this," he snaps.

Dad's expression darkens and he moves to stand in front of Nick. "Don't talk to her like that," he says, his voice hard and menacing. I've never heard him sound like that, even at his angriest.

Nick steps forward again, bringing him just inches from my father's tense frame. They're pretty evenly matched in size, but Dad's quiet, simmering anger feels more dangerous than Nick's hair-trigger temper. I immediately regret my comment. As mad as I am at my father, the last thing I want is for him to get hurt. Especially not here, where we're completely isolated from society.

"I can talk however I damn well want," Nick snarls. "You might be Russell's pet right now, but that doesn't mean you're the boss around here. You'll never be the boss, because you're just a spineless know-it-all whose only skill is swinging a hammer."

I watch, heart pounding, as Dad's fists clench and he takes a step forward. Nick instinctively moves aside and almost trips over poor Max, who'd gotten up to sit beside him. The near fall enrages Nick even more, and he quickly rights himself before facing my father again, hands raised. But before he can do anything, push or punch or whatever else he had in mind, Charlene darts forward and edges herself between them.

"Enough," she says firmly, like she's breaking up a playground fight between two kids. "Just walk away from each other."

This seems to snap Dad out of his fury. He glances around the lodge like he's reminding himself of where he is, and that April and I are here too, watching everything unfold. His hands unclench and he takes a breath, steadying himself. Nick, still poised to fight, doesn't flinch as my father turns to meet his icy glare one last time.

"Stay away from me," he says, low and calm. "And stay away from my children. Or else I'll run you out of here myself."

Before Nick can respond, the door swings open and Dennis steps inside, dressed in a rain jacket and tall rubber boots. "What's going on in here?" he demands, pulling off his hood. "I could hear the yelling from the parking lot."

"Nothing," Dad says, taking a step back. "Just a little disagreement."

"Disagreement?" Nick spins toward Dennis while pointing an angry finger at my father. "He just threatened me."

Dennis wipes his boots on the mat and moves toward the living room, his eyes on Nick. "This isn't how we resolve issues around here. If two people have a difference of opinion, then they need to figure out a way to talk it through calmly and rationally."

"Why are you looking at *me*? It's Gabe who refuses to listen to reason."

"Now, Nick—" Dennis lifts a hand as if to place it on Nick's shoulder, but Nick jerks away from him, his face so red it's practically purple.

"Of course. Take *his* side." Nick gestures toward my father again. "He's the one who's earned your respect, right?"

Dad turns away like he's heard enough and motions for me to follow him. I obey without hesitation. As we head for the door, I meet Dane's sympathetic gaze while Dad holds out a hand to April, who's now huddled against Kiana's side, confused and scared. We've never seen our father clash with another person like that, and it's left us both a little stunned.

"Come on, Sunshine," he says gruffly.

April immediately takes his hand. As we head for the door, I glance back at Nick. He meets my eyes for a moment, then he walks away too, snapping his fingers so Max will follow.

Chapter Twenty

I spend the next afternoon on the porch of our cabin, sitting in an Adirondack chair and reading one of my paperbacks. Every few paragraphs, I check on April, who's playing with the son of a family who arrived this morning. The ranch's population almost doubled this weekend, with members dropping in to take advantage of the grounds. Groups of smiling, chattering people have been passing by the cabins all day, carrying fishing rods and tackle boxes or riding bicycles. It's like the pictures on the ranch's website come to life.

April was introduced to Lincoln, a boy about her age, when his parents stopped to chat with the family staying in the cabin next to ours. That was over two hours ago, and they've been inseparable ever since.

April kicks a soccer ball toward Lincoln, who blocks the "goal"—two large rocks positioned a few feet apart on the grass. It's nice not to have to entertain her for a while. I turn my attention back to my book. I'm so engrossed in an action scene, I don't notice my father approaching the cabin until he's almost at the porch. He climbs the steps slowly, like he's carrying an invisible weight on his back.

"You're late today," I say, my eyes on the page.

"Ran into some issues."

He brushes dirt off his clothes and goes inside. Twenty minutes later he reappears, freshly showered and armed with a bottle of beer. I haven't moved from my chair. He sits in the one next to mine and balances his bottle on the splintery arm.

"I'm glad she found a friend here," he says, gazing at April and Lincoln, now playing leapfrog on the grass.

"Me too." Though Lincoln and his family are going home at some point tonight, and April will be back to being bored by tomorrow. Still, I know she misses playing with her friends at home, so it's nice to see her laughing and happy.

Dad downs half his beer in two long gulps, then sets it on the chair arm again. "So. About what happened yesterday."

I stop reading and look at him expectantly.

"Jodi needs someone to help out in the stables. She won't be around tomorrow, but I told her you'd be by first thing Tuesday morning."

"What?" I'd assumed he was going to apologize for humiliating me in front of everyone and almost punching Nick, even if he did deserve it. "Why would I do that?"

"You disappeared after breakfast yesterday without saying a word. You left April when you knew I needed you to watch her. You had me running all over the place, worried sick that you were hurt or lost." He rattles off each transgression like he's been keeping a list. "Actions have consequences, Isobel. And I can't exactly ground you here, so—"

"So instead you'll punish me by forcing me to participate in ranch chores?" I close the book and toss it on the porch beside my chair. "Can't I pick cucumbers or something? I don't know anything about horses."

"You don't need to know anything to clean up after them."

"What am I supposed to do with April while I'm mucking out stalls or whatever?" The idea of me shoveling horseshit for the woman who's crushing on my father makes me want to laugh. Or vomit.

"She can ride that horse she likes. Look," he says in a gentler tone. "I think you'd be happier here if you got more involved. Everyone is expected to do their part around the ranch."

"But what's the point in me getting involved now? We're leaving in a few days."

He's silent for a moment, his gaze on the copse of trees in the distance. "That's another thing. I was talking to Russell earlier."

"And?" I ask, my guard already up.

"There are some structural problems with the new shelter," he says, taking another drink of beer. "It's going to take a little longer than the builders originally planned, so he asked me to stay on for an extra week to help out."

No is my first thought. "An extra week? Dad, we're supposed to leave a week from tomorrow. That was the plan."

Images of home flash through my mind. My room. My bed. My town. Mom's car. Claire. My chest aches at the thought of being here for even one day longer, let alone an entire week. No. I've gone along with a lot so far, but this is too much.

"Plans change." He gestures around us, at the expanse of green, the forest, the beautifully constructed porch we're currently sitting on. "Being here isn't exactly a hardship, is it?"

"You told me two weeks. You *promised*." Familiar panic swirls in my gut, even though I'm outside where there's space for miles.

"No," he says, his voice getting softer as mine rises. "I said we'd wait and see how it goes, and this is how it's going. They need me for a little while longer."

"*We* need you, Dad. April and me. We need you at home."

He looks at me, his eyes tired. "Please, Isobel. It's just one more week."

My fingers find Mom's silver *always* bracelet on my wrist. I run my thumb over the stamped letters, trying to draw comfort from them. From my mom. What would she do, if she were here?

Only she *wouldn't* be here. She wouldn't have let it get this far.

Thoughts of my mom shift into images of Jodi and my father, laughing together.

"Does this have anything to do with *her*?" I ask.

Dad frowns. "Who?"

I don't bother saying her name. "You think I didn't notice you two flirting at breakfast yesterday?"

"What are you talking about?" he asks, but his face goes red, betraying him. "I wasn't—there's nothing—"

I stand up, my hand clenched. "You know, even though Mom's been gone two years, you're still married to her. Or at least that's how I think of you. Then again, you don't seem to care *what* I think anymore."

He reaches out to touch my arm, but I dodge him and step away. "I'm going for a walk. Is that still allowed?"

Not waiting for an answer, I thump down the steps to the grass and start moving, not even caring which direction I go as long as it's away from our cabin.

I keep walking until I reach the edge of the woods and enter the first trail opening I come across, barely noticing the uneven ground under my flip-flops. Less than two minutes in, my foot sinks into a crater and I fall, landing flat on my ass on the pointy rocks. Pain rockets through me, which only intensifies my fury. Eyes watering, I pick up a rock and throw it as hard as I can into the trees. It lands with a soft, unsatisfying plunk, so I throw another one. Then another. Until finally, my fingers close around something different. Something smooth and cool.

It's another rock, but it's not big and jagged like the others. This one is oval-shaped and about the size of a walnut, grayish black with thin lines of silver running through it. I turn it over on my hands. The surface isn't completely smooth, and it's dirty, but this doesn't stop me from seeing the possibilities. With a long soak in soapy water and a few hours of sanding, this stone could make a beautiful centerpiece for a necklace.

A design starts taking shape in my head—a polished stone pendant held in place with macramé netting and a box knot, suspended on a black nylon cord. I haven't made any jewelry since I got here, but now, sitting here on the ground, my fingers itch to create something again, to feel taut string against my fingertips and smell the pungent scent of glue. Making jewelry has always been soothing for me, a way to center myself and untangle my thoughts. I could use that around here.

I scramble to my feet again, then slip the stone into my pocket as I walk carefully out of the woods. The anger from before has been dulled by a surge of creativity.

"Damn, what happened to you?"

Dane's voice jolts me out of my head. He's walking across the grass, his phone in hand. Crap. I probably look like a wreck.

"Nothing, why?"

He stops in front of me. "Well, you're limping."

I peer down at my ankle. It's sore, but I can still walk on it okay. "I'm fine," I say. "I just...fell in the woods."

"Oh." He frowns at me for a moment, like he's wondering if I hit my head in there too.

I glance at his phone. "Did you manage to get service here?"

"Ha. No." He slips it in his shorts pocket. "But if I'm lucky, I can get two seconds of connection when I'm standing near that shrub over there."

"Most people just go to the lodge."

He gazes in that direction. The sound of voices and laughter drift toward us, along with the faint whiff of barbecue smoke. "I don't really like hanging out there. Too crowded."

I nod and brush the dirt off my behind. "I haven't seen you around since...um, after the store yesterday."

"Oh, I've been busy. My mom and I were taking groups on hikes through the woods to show them which plants and mushrooms are safe to eat." He stuffs his hands in his pockets. "So, what happened with Nick and your dad yesterday...that was intense. Are you okay?"

I shrug, not really in the mood to talk about it. I'm still trying to wrap my mind around the fact that even with people like Nick around, my father believes this ranch is a safer alternative to home.

"Nick's gone completely off the rails," Dane says. "I think he'd hide the ranch under a giant dome if he could figure out how to build one."

When I laugh, he looks at the ground with a small, pleased smile on his face. It's really cute. My heart gives a little flutter.

"So, your parents are members now?" I ask, slapping a mosquito off my arm. "Nick mentioned that Dad was the only visitor left."

He looks up again, his hair tumbling over his face. "Yeah, they joined a few days ago. They've started looking for a place for us in Holcomb."

He says it like it's no big thing, though I know it can't be easy to pick up everything and move to a strange place. But I get the sense that he doesn't want to talk about it, so I let it go.

After a long, silent pause, Dane tips his face to the sky. "It's a nice evening. You know where you can get the best view of the sunset?" When I shake my head, he says, "The guard tower. I've been up there a couple times. You want to check it out?"

I glance in the direction of our cabin. When we first got here, my father warned us against going up in the guard tower, that it's not intended as a place to play. He'd probably freak if he knew I climbed up there, especially since it's getting dark.

I look back at Dane. The way he's watching me sends a spark of heat through my body. "Okay."

We walk along the perimeter of the woods, not talking much. The sun has dipped below the trees, but it's not so dark that we can't make out the tower and wooden ladder rising up through the branches. When Dane motions for me to climb up first, I hesitate.

"It's safe," he assures me. When I still don't move, he says, "Okay, I'll go up first."

He starts climbing, fast and sure. When he's about halfway up, I take a deep breath and follow him, my movements much less confident. A light breeze ruffles my hair and cools my sweaty neck as I put more and more space between my body and the ground. I pause on every rung, making sure my still-tender ankle is secure before I climb to the next one. By the time I reach the top, Dane is waiting. He reaches down into the opening in the floor, and I let go of the last rung and grip his hands instead. He pulls, and suddenly I'm standing in a mini log cabin, suspended in the trees.

"Wow," I say, looking around. The interior is about eight-feet-squared, with a built-in bench along one wall and a small window on the other. The forest-facing side has a door leading out onto a wrap-around platform with a railing. That must be where the armed guard would patrol, on alert for approaching marauders.

Dane ducks outside onto the platform. I take another fortifying breath and join him, my stomach dropping as I realize how far up we actually are. From here, we can see the lodge, the gravel road leading to the ranch's entrance, and even a glimpse of the far-off highway through the treetops.

"The sun sets on the other side," Dane says, brushing past me. I follow, keeping as far away from the railing as possible.

When I turn the corner, I immediately understand why he brought me up here. From this side of the tower, we have a wide, unobstructed view of the horizon. The sun is slowly sinking toward it, a glowing ball of fire against a pink-and-orange-streaked sky.

"It's beautiful," I say, even though *beautiful* is not nearly a strong enough word for this view.

"I know," he replies softly.

When I turn to him, he's not looking at the sunset. He's looking right at me.

"Dane," I say, swallowing hard. We're standing so close I can feel the warmth coming off his skin. My pulse is racing.

"Yeah?" he asks, his gaze dropping to my lips.

I don't know what to say next, or even if I'm capable of forming words. So instead, I lean in and kiss him, surprising us both. He kisses me back, his arms sliding around my waist as mine circle his neck, bringing us closer. Heat blooms in my stomach and quickly spreads through the rest of my body, making me feel like I'm about to float off the edge of the tower. I cling to him even tighter, my fingers entwined in his hair.

I'm not sure where this surge of boldness is coming from. Maybe it's being up here with him, perched in the trees, like we're in an entirely different place. Not on Endurance Ranch, with its shelters and stockpiles and doomsday panic, but somewhere peaceful and new. A place where I can look out and see the rest of the world, spread wide open in front of me.

Chapter Twenty-one

"Watch me, Izzie!" April calls from the corral. She's perched on Misty's sleek back, all smiles, wearing her new riding boots and helmet, both compliments of Jodi the Horse Lady. Jodi walks closely alongside her, making sure she's secure in case Misty gets spooked by a chicken or something random as they slowly circle the corral.

"I'm watching," I call back from the open barn, where I'm sweeping the aisle with a push broom and trying not to pass out from the midday heat. The other horses doze in their stalls on either side of me, only perking up to snort at me as I pass. A giant white horse with brown spots stamps its feet at me as I clean up piles of shavings and straw in front of his stall.

As far as punishments go, I guess it could be worse. Instead of cleaning horse equipment and sweeping the barn, Jodi could have asked me to sift through stalls for manure.

I peer outside again, watching as she repositions April on the saddle. I can see why my father might be attracted to her, or at least flattered by her interest in him. Mom was

The End of Always

pretty too, with her carefully applied makeup and jewelry, but Jodi is beautiful in a natural, effortless way. She's probably the type whose morning beauty routine is throwing her hair in a braid and splashing cold water on her face.

A stab of pain shoots through my right hand, distracting me. In the dim light of the barn, I see a long sliver of wood sticking out of my palm. I rest the broom's stupid splintery handle against the wall and try to dig out the sliver with my fingernails.

"Looking fierce up there, Sunshine."

I lift my head again and see my father, smiling as he approaches the corral. April gives him a quick wave and grins even wider. Jodi does the same, even though he's a sweaty mess with his clothes covered in wood dust and his arms and hands smeared with dirt. She doesn't seem to mind.

Dad's gaze bounces to me as I exit the barn, still nursing my stinging palm. "How's it going?" he asks, resting his arms on top of the fence.

He's clearly talking to me, but Jodi answers. "She's been a big help today. She spent the morning polishing tack, and now she's dealing with the mess Cyclone made in there."

I assume Cyclone is the brown-spotted horse. Fitting.

"Good." He grips the fence and leans back. "Well, I just wanted to stop by to see how everyone was coming along. You can take April back to the cabin after you're finished, Isobel. I'm sure Jodi has other things to do today."

Jodi guides the horse to a stop near where my father is standing. "No, not really. I mean, when I'm not in my office, you'll usually find me here."

I examine their body language for some kind of clue. Had something already happened between them? Would it be obvious? Like, if someone looked at Dane and me, would they be able to tell that something happened between *us* the other night?

My heat-cooked body grows even warmer as memories of the guard tower flood through me. I'm so sidetracked, I almost miss seeing April dismounting the horse and wrapping her arms around Jodi, hugging her like she does after every ride. I avert my eyes, focusing on my splinter again. I'm glad April gets along so well here, but that doesn't mean I like watching her bond with Jodi.

"I can't believe how fast she's taken to riding," Jodi says as she opens the gate for April. "Just let me know if you ever want a turn up there, Izzie."

"It's Isobel," I correct her, my tone icy. Dad shoots me a look as Jodi's smile slips a couple of notches.

"Can I come back tomorrow?" April asks as she takes off her helmet.

"Of course," Jodi says before turning to my father. "Don't forget about the party Thursday night, okay?"

April's face lights up. "We're having a party?"

Jodi's grin goes full force again. "The second Thursday of every month, Russell throws a wine and cheese party in the gazebo for members. I was telling your dad about it the other day. It's always a fun night."

A wine and cheese party? How bougie. If Jodi knew my father at all, she'd realize that he's more of a beer-and-nuts-at-home kind of guy. No way will he agree to sip wine and nibble cheese in the gazebo.

"We'll be there," he says.

His response feels like a gut punch. Maybe *I'm* the one who doesn't know him at all.

Dad and April head to the store after dinner, so I'm alone in the cabin when Dane knocks on the screen door.

"You want to go for a walk?" he asks. "I found a spot the other day that I wanted to show you."

My heart skips. I saw him earlier today on the way back from the barn, but April was with me and I smelled like horses and leather polish, so all we did was wave. Only in the evenings can we truly be alone, and even then, time is limited. Dad is fine with me spending time with Dane—he thinks he's a "good kid"—but that doesn't mean he approves of me wandering around in the dark with him at all hours.

I meet Dane's eyes again. His dark gaze burns into mine.

"Sure," I say, grabbing my flip-flops.

"You should probably wear sneakers."

I raise one brow, intrigued, but he just smiles enigmatically.

Five minutes later, he's leading me past the log homes to the entrance of a hiking trail I haven't seen before. Probably because, unlike the other trails, there's no gravel or well-trampled dirt to mark the pathway. This one is narrow and untamed; the only thing that gives it away as a walkable trail is a slight gap in the vegetation.

A few minutes later, I'm grateful to be wearing my pink Vans and not my flip-flops. The ground is uneven and occasionally swampy, dotted with thorny bushes that make me wish I wore pants too.

"You okay?" Dane asks, glancing back at me. He, of course, is as sure-footed in here as the wildlife that's surely lurking in the trees.

I duck as something the size of a golf ball buzzes past my face. "Yep."

After walking for what feels like ages—though it's probably been about fifteen minutes—I hear the distinct sound of rushing water to our right. A few minutes later, the trail curves toward a narrow, bubbling stream snaking through the woods. We follow it for a few yards, then step out into a rocky clearing. A blanket of cold mist coats my face and I gasp. The stream we've been following has expanded into a small pool of water that looks like it was scooped out of the earth. Above it, rivulets of water trickle off an outcrop of rocks and into the pool below.

"I came across it the other day when I was in here looking for fiddleheads," Dane says over the sound of the rippling water. "The heat was killing me, so I jumped in there to cool off. It's too shallow for swimming, but the water's nice and clean." He grins at me, backing away. "What do you think? You want to try it? Don't worry, I made sure it's safe."

My gaze shifts to the clear, inviting water. The live-in-the-moment part of me that I thought was dead and buried suddenly pokes its head up again at Dane's hopeful face.

"I guess I'll have to trust you."

He grins and pulls his shirt over his head, tossing it on one of the larger rocks. For a moment, I'm sidetracked by the sight of his bare skin, smooth and toned and bronzed even deeper by the sun. I've seen him shirtless since we've been here, but never this close up, and not since our relationship progressed to kissing. It takes me a few seconds to tear my eyes away so I can untie my Vans.

I'm too self-conscious to take off anything more than my shoes, so I step up to the pool in my shorts and tank top. When the water hits my skin, I stifle a squeal. It's a lot colder than I anticipated.

"You get used to it," Dane assures me from the middle of the pool, which only comes up to his waist. As I slowly wade out to him, he falls backward, dunking himself under the water. "You just need to do that," he adds when he surfaces again, rubbing a hand over his face.

"No, thanks." I continue toward him, my arms crossed over my chest.

"I miss swimming. This is the first summer in years that I haven't gone to the pool even once. Kind of makes it hard to practice for swim team tryouts in the fall."

"Aren't you homeschooled?" I ask, stopping in front of him.

He laughs. "Homeschooled kids do sports too. Not all teams are school-based."

"I've never joined a team in my life, so I wouldn't know. My best friend Claire is a jock though. She's into soccer."

"And what are you into?"

My gaze travels down his arm to his hand, resting just under the water. "I make jewelry," I say, uncrossing my arms to touch the hemp bracelet on his wrist.

"Really?" Dane says, capturing my hand in his. "How did I not know this about you?"

I shrug. "You never asked."

He detangles his fingers from mine and places his hands on my waist, his thumbs brushing the exposed skin above my shorts. His hands feel warm despite the numbing chill of the water. As he leans in to kiss me, I try not to think about the fact that this is all temporary. That maybe I shouldn't be getting close to a boy who I may never see again. I try not to think about anything but the warmth of his mouth and the feel of his hair between my fingers, and how being with him is the only thing that makes me forget where I really am. Like the other night in the guard tower, *here* doesn't feel like part of the ranch. *Here* is a private little oasis, created especially for us.

"Damn," Dane mumbles when our lips detach several minutes later. "I wish I wasn't leaving on Friday."

I pull back. "What?"

He raises his eyebrows. "Well, yeah. We can't stay at the ranch forever. I mean, unless there's a declared emergency. You knew that, right?"

I fold my arms over my chest, suddenly cold again, and start wading toward the edge of the pool. The sun has disappeared behind the canopy of trees, cloaking our little oasis in shadows. "We should probably leave before it gets too dark to find the path."

"Oh," he says, and I can hear his disappointment. "Is everything okay?"

I don't want to tell him I don't want him to leave. Or that he's the only part of this place that feels anything close to normal. So instead, I say, "My father will probably send out a search party if we don't get back soon."

"Right."

Once we're back on the rocks, I try to keep the conversation going. "Where will you go next?"

"Not far. We're parking the Winnebago at this campground about thirty miles down the road and staying there until we find a place to live. Don't worry," he adds, flashing me a grin as he slips his shirt back on. "I plan to come back here every day to visit. I'll have the car."

"I'm not worried, I—" Lost for words, I lean over to tie my Vans, not wanting him to see how much I dread the thought of being here without him. "I guess I assumed you were sticking around a little longer."

"Hey," he said, nudging me, "I wish I was." We start walking, falling into step beside each other even though the path is really only wide enough for one. "I heard my moms talking the other night. They said your dad has an open-ended invitation to stay here."

"Because of the shelter construction," I say.

"And because Russell likes him. He's exactly the type of person they want at this place."

"What type is that?"

He pushes aside a tree branch so it doesn't whip against our faces. "Smart, logical, level-headed...you know, the opposite of Nick."

I snort. So it's not just me who noticed Russell's apathy toward the ranch's resident hothead. "Nick's a member, though, and my father is not."

"True," he says, taking my hand as I navigate past a muddy patch. "But I bet Russell has been putting pressure on him to join. I mean, he needs people like your father to give the ranch purpose and keep it running. This place might be a survival community, but it's also—"

"A business," I finish for him. "I get it."

He nods. "And your dad's skills are good for business."

Chapter Twenty-two

I assumed kids would be exempt from the gazebo wine and cheese party, so I'm surprised when my father announces at dinner that we'll all be attending this evening's event.

"Is it mandatory?" I ask, standing up and carrying my empty plate to the sink.

"No," Dad says, doing the same. "But I think it would be nice to get out and mix with the community."

I want to ask why it matters, seeing as we'll soon be leaving the *community*, but things have been okay between us these last couple of days—aside from the low buzz of tension that's been constant since we left home—and I don't want to ruin it now.

"I want some cheese, Izzie," April says, poking at her uneaten broccoli.

I guess that settles it, then. We're going to this party.

An hour later, the three of us are walking toward the lodge area, Dad in jeans and a button-up and April and I in the sundresses we haven't worn until now. It's not the best night for an outdoor gathering—dark clouds blanket the sky, and the wind is picking up by the minute. Maybe I'll get lucky and this thing will be cut short.

The gathering is in full swing when we arrive. Clusters of people stand around on the grass in front of the gazebo, holding wine glasses or beer bottles or cubes of cheese on toothpicks. The gazebo, strewn with small white lights, is taken up by two long tables. One for the drinks—wine and beer for the adults, grape juice and apple cider for the underage—and one for the platters of various cheeses. The extravagant scene seems odd against the rustic backdrop of the ranch.

I glance around for Dane and his parents, but my search is interrupted by Dennis and Roberta, who intercept us on our way to the gazebo. Dennis is commanding as usual in his beige Endurance Ranch shirt, and Roberta—hair sleek and shiny and wearing heels instead of rubber boots—looks more like I remember her from the first time we met.

"Gabe." Dennis steps forward and shakes Dad's hand, his face flushed and beaming. "Good to see you."

I look past them, half-expecting Nick to appear and start antagonizing my father or yammering about the wall again. Then I spot him in the gazebo, piling cheese cubes onto a napkin and not even looking in our direction.

"You girls look pretty," Roberta says to April and me.

April smiles and gazes down at her yellow-and-white striped jersey dress, which makes her look extra sunshiny. I'm wearing the only dress I packed—a white floral cami style with spaghetti straps and a flared skirt. I even put smoothing serum in my hair and did my makeup, two things I haven't bothered with since I got here.

Roberta and Dennis walk with us to the gazebo, where Dad and Dennis grab beers while Roberta picks over the cheese and I pour two glasses of cider. Back out on the grass, I scan the yard for Dane again. This time I spot him, walking past the lodge with his moms, hands tucked into the front pockets of his shorts. He sees me at the same time, and a slow smile spreads across his face as he takes in my appearance. He's used to seeing me in shorts and comfy tops, hair in a ponytail, and face makeup-free. Suddenly I'm glad I decided to put in an effort.

"I think it's going to rain," Roberta says, frowning at the sky. It's even darker now, like dusk has already fallen even though it's still at least an hour away.

Dennis takes a drink of beer. "If it does, we'll just move everything into the lodge. Too bad the new shelter isn't complete yet, because a party would be a great way to break it in, wouldn't it? Oh, that reminds me," he adds, turning to my father. "Jodi told me the good news, Gabe. I'm surprised you're not sporting the logo tonight." He taps the jaguar head over the pocket of his shirt.

What? My head snaps toward my father, but he keeps his eyes on Dennis, his expression as controlled as ever. But his fingers tighten around his beer bottle, and I know he feels the weight of my stare.

"Oh. Well..." is all he says to Dennis's comment. He takes a swig of beer and shoots me a look that I decipher immediately: He's sorry he didn't tell me before, but this isn't the time or place to discuss it.

"We're so glad to have you all," Dennis says, his gaze sweeping over the three of us. "A community is only as good as its members."

The apple cider turns sour in my stomach, and I spin and walk away, not caring if I'm being rude. I place my empty glass on a table in the gazebo and head straight for Dane, who's standing with his parents and a couple of others at the other end of the lawn. Seeing me, he detaches himself from the group to meet me halfway.

"Hey," he says, his dark eyes skimming over me from my hair to my bare calves. "You look incredible."

"Do you want to get out of here?" I ask without any preamble. Right now, I don't trust myself not to make a scene.

"Um," he says, glancing back at his parents. "I don't think—"

"It's okay, never mind." Impatient, I back away from him and start walking again. Ahead, my father is still stationed in front of the gazebo, only now he's chatting with Jodi, who looks gorgeous in a strapless blue sundress, her hair loose and cascading over her bare shoulders. April stands slightly behind them, downing another cup of cider. None of them notice me as I pass.

"Isobel! Wait." Dane catches up to me again, falling into step beside me as I cross the lawn and head toward the log homes. "What's wrong?"

"Nothing. Everything," I say, spitting the words past my tight throat. A raindrop hits my arm, then another one, but the sensation barely registers. "My father went and joined the ranch, and now he's over there flirting with the horse lady. Other than that, things are fantastic."

Dane, having already witnessed me in rage mode, just listens quietly.

"And he didn't even *tell* me," I continue, pulling open the door to my cabin. "I found out from *Dennis*. I'm so *sick* of being in the dark all the time. I'm sick of my father just deciding things without even considering how April and I feel about it."

Dane takes my hand and leads me over to the couch. He sits and pulls me down beside him, keeping his fingers wrapped around mine. It's dark in here, much darker than it usually is at this time of day, but neither of us bothers to turn on a light.

"I'm sick of being *here*." Hot tears gather in my eyes. "I just want to go home."

His arm slides around my shoulders, and I lean into him, resting my head on his shoulder. I can't believe I'm crying on him again. He must think I'm unhinged.

"I know it doesn't seem like it right now," he says, smoothing back my hair with his free hand, "but everything is going to be okay."

"I used to feel that way. Believe it or not, I'm usually the optimistic type."

"I can see that. I mean, not right this second, but...."

I snort and sit up. When I wipe my eyes, my fingers come away stained with black. Guess my eye makeup is ruined. I grab a paper towel from the kitchen, then sit down next to him again. "Jesus," I say, pressing the paper towel to my face. "I must look like such a mess."

"No." He reaches up and rubs his thumb over a spot I missed on my cheekbone. "You look beautiful. You always do."

Now I laugh for real. "You know, no one's ever told me that before. A guy who's not related to me, I mean. I've never had a boyfriend. I've never even been on a date."

"I find that hard to believe."

"Well, it's true." I toss the soggy paper towel onto the coffee table. "When my mom died, I kind of...withdrew into myself. All the dating drama at school seemed trivial after that, so I kind of lost interest in the whole romance thing."

Dane pulls back a bit. "And now?"

"Now...." I take his hand, nudging him closer again. "I'm definitely interested again."

The air shifts between us, and suddenly I don't care what I look like or what happened outside or in the past or anywhere else. All that matters is this moment, the two of us sitting close in the near-dark. The feel of his breath on my face as he leans in to kiss me. The quickening of my pulse as his hand skims over the bare skin on my back. All I want is to get lost in him, to pretend, just for a while, that I'm somewhere else—anywhere else—but here.

Reality crashes in again when the door swings open and the cabin is flooded with light. Squinting against the brightness, I untangle myself from Dane and look at my father, who's standing in the doorway, dripping wet and staring at us.

"Isobel," he says sharply.

I quickly straighten the hem of my dress and glance at Dane, who looks as mortified as I feel. "Dad, we—"

"Is April here?" he cuts in, and suddenly I realize the expression on his face is not anger, but fear. "Is she with you?"

I stare back at him, confused. "What? No, she's—I left her with you."

He swallows and looks behind him to the still-open door. When I follow his gaze, I'm surprised to see that it's pitch-black and pouring outside, sheets of rain pounding against the boards of the porch and the window beside us. I never even noticed.

"Dad?" A bolt of panic runs through me and I scramble to my feet. "What do you mean? She's *not* with you?"

He turns back to me, his eyes frantic. "When the rain started, everyone was running around trying to move everything into the lodge. It got really chaotic for a minute, and I—when I looked around for April, she was gone."

Gone. The word is barely out of his mouth before my feet start moving, hurling me toward the open doorway and out into the storm.

Chapter Twenty-three

I don't realize Dane is right beside me until he touches my arm. "I'll grab our waterproof flashlight and check the woods."

Oh God, the woods, my brain screams as he disappears into the dark. My father, having checked in and around the cabin, heads back to the lodge, his shoes kicking up water as he runs. Now I'm alone on the squelchy grass, my body tense but my mind unable to decide where to start. We're on sixty-acre property backed up against a fifteen-thousand-acre forest. She could be anywhere.

A horrible thought hits me, turning my blood to ice. *The guard tower.*

I bolt in that direction, swiping rain from my eyes as my mind churns out one dreadful image after another. April, slipping on the ladder and falling. April, walking out onto the platform, too close to the edge. April, her little body lying on the ground. April, broken and hurt, or worse.

Relief almost doubles me over when I get to the base of the tower and don't see her anywhere. Still, I scale it quickly—at least twice as fast as the first time I did it—my fear for my sister overriding my fear of heights. She's not inside either, so I climb back down and circle the perimeter of the field, screaming her name into the driving rain until my throat is raw.

She's always been a runner, but she knows better than to take off on her own without telling anyone. Unless she didn't take off...unless someone...no. I can't even contemplate that.

Not knowing what else to do or where else to look, I make my way to the lodge. The rain has tapered into a foggy mist, making it hard to see much of anything. Only once I'm a few feet from the building can I make out several people standing around in front, some wearing hooded rain jackets. Dad comes running up from the opposite side, flashlight in one hand. Our eyes meet, desperation passing through the fog between us, and I shake my head. Dad's face collapses, and it hits me that I've never seen him this scared. Even during the hurricane years ago. Even when Mom got her diagnosis.

"She's not by the shelter construction," he says, panting hard. I move to stand next to him, my fingers gripping the sodden fabric at the back of his shirt.

Nick appears then, accompanied by a dripping wet Max. "She's not at the gardens, either," he announces. After what happened between him and my father, I'm surprised he's even bothered joining the search.

"Dennis and I checked every inch of the lodge," Roberta says. "She's definitely not in there."

I turn to my father. "We have to call the police."

"No," Nick says quickly. "The last thing we need is a bunch of cops poking around."

Russell steps in closer and pulls off his hood. "Nick's right. Let's not jump the gun here. The little girl couldn't have gotten very far."

White hot anger rips through me. "That *little girl* is my sister," I snarl at him. "Her name is April Julianna McCarthy. She's six years old and she's somewhere out there, all alone and probably scared out of her mind." I shift my glare to Nick, who's watching me with his cold blue eyes. "So it's not up to you to decide what *we* need."

A hand squeezes my shoulder, easing me back. "Isobel."

I shake out of the grasp and spin around. It's Dane, his hair dripping and his T-shirt plastered to his skin. I search his face for news, even though I know there isn't any. He didn't find her either. All the fight goes out of me, and I crumble into his arms and completely fall apart.

"There!"

Dennis's booming voice cuts through the muted chatter. He's pointing at something in the distance. My heart in my throat, I break away from Dane and turn around, following everyone's gaze. Someone is approaching from the direction of the farm area, a slim figure with long curly hair carrying a smaller curly-haired someone on her hip.

"I found her!" the person calls, and for a moment—a crazy, fleeting moment—I think it's my mother. But then someone shines a flashlight on her, and I realize it's Jodi, her long hair twisted from the rain. And in her arms is April, soaked and crying and clinging to her neck like she's afraid to let go.

Relief turns my legs to water, and for a moment all I can do is watch as Dad rushes to meet them, scooping April out of Jodi's arms and into his. April wraps herself around him as the three of them join the rest of the group.

"I found her," Jodi repeats, out of breath. Her blue sundress is drenched and streaked with dirt. "She was in the stables hiding behind the hay bales next to Misty's stall. She said she was worried there was going to be a tornado, and she thought the horses might be scared."

April lets out a sob into Dad's shoulder. "I'm sorry."

Feeling returns to my legs, and I run to them, pressing my face into April's damp curls. Dad transfers her to me, and I hug her tightly, my heart hammering in my ears. Finally, I set her down on the ground and take hold of her shoulders, my eyes scanning her for injuries. Finding nothing but dirt and mud, I focus on her puffy face. Then, to my surprise, a different kind of anger engulfs me.

"April, what were you *thinking*?" I hiss, still gripping her shoulders. "You can't run away like that, you could've gotten hurt. We were so worried. Don't you *ever* do that again, do you understand me?"

Her bottom lip trembles, and she twists out of my grasp. I watch, helpless, as she runs directly to Jodi and burrows into her side like she's scared of me. My father moves to stand next to them and places his hand on April's head. The sight of the three them, huddled together like a little family, makes my chest ache.

I got her back safe tonight, but it still feels like I'm losing her. Losing them both.

It takes a while to get April to sleep. Once all is quiet from our bedroom, Dad quietly shuts the door and joins me in the living room, where I've been sitting for the past half hour, too exhausted to move.

"We need to talk," he says, sitting in the chair across from me. He looks exhausted too, like he aged ten years in the past two hours. "What happened tonight should never have happened. Isobel, I count on you to keep an eye on your sister and make sure she's safe."

I can't believe what I'm hearing. "Dad, I left her with *you*. I wasn't even there when she ran off by herself."

"That's exactly my point."

"April is *your* child, not mine. It's not my fault she got lost because I wasn't there to watch her every move." I cross my arms. "Since we got here, all I've *done* is watch April."

His mouth twists. "Clearly that's not all you've been doing."

I feel a twinge of embarrassment. "God, we were just kissing. Dane is the only person I can talk to around here. I'm not going to apologize for spending time with him."

"The only person you can talk to?" he repeats, frowning. "That's not fair, Isobel. I know I've been gone a lot, but you know you can always talk to me about anything."

"Right. Except you never listen to what I say." I sit up, my tiredness forgotten. "You knew I didn't want to come here, but you dragged me here anyway. You told me two weeks, then you pushed it to three. *You* said this was just a visit to see if the ranch worked for us as a family, but then you didn't bother to ask our opinions about it before you went and bought a membership." I pause to take a breath. When I speak again, my voice is quiet. "When were you going to tell me?"

"Soon," he says, dropping his gaze to the floor. "Tomorrow. I'm still trying to figure some things out."

"Things like what? A place to live? Because I won't move here. I agreed to three weeks, but I'll never agree to that."

He meets my eyes again, his expression hardening. "You have no idea how much work I've put into this place since we got here. I can't just walk away now. This community is the answer for us—"

"No, it's the answer for *you*. You think you're protecting us by stashing us away in the middle of nowhere, but even a twenty-foot wall can't save us from everything." Tears sting my eyes, and I blink them away. "April thought a tornado was coming tonight, so she ran. Why do you think she did that? Kids aren't dumb; they pick up on things. You taught her to run away and hide when she gets scared, just like you did by bringing us here."

He rubs his hands over his face and shakes his head, like he's trying to dislodge my words, wipe them away. But I'm not going to let him, not anymore.

"You think you're taking control by preparing us, but you can't control the future, Dad. You don't have the power to save us from every terrible thing that might happen." I swallow and look away, toward the blackness outside the windows. "You couldn't save Mom, and you can't save us."

"That's out of line, Isobel," he says, his voice booming in the small, insulated space. "Everything I do is to protect you and April. You don't have to agree with my choices or even understand them, but you do have to trust that I'm doing what I think is best for my family."

"Our family," I yell back at him. "This is *our* family, Dad. Or what's left of it, anyway."

The pressure behind my eyes finally breaks, and the tears that have been hovering spill down my cheeks. I wipe them away impatiently, still focused on my father's weary face.

"What happened to you?" I ask, shaking my head. "Three years ago, you never would have considered moving away from the house we grew up in. And you wouldn't have done what you did tonight, either, standing back and saying nothing while Nick and Russell shot down my idea of calling the police."

"Isobel, you don't know what you're—"

"And what about Jodi?" I cut him off. There's no use in dancing around this part.

He averts his gaze. "What about her?"

His refusal to look me in the eye gives me my answer, and the thought of him moving on here of all places is so painful that all I want to do is hurt him back. "Do you think Mom would be okay with you replacing her with some woman you just met at a doomsday prepper ranch?"

His face flushes red, and he jumps up from his chair. "How dare you—"

A small, breathy sob stops him. April is standing at the entrance to the hallway, her crocodile clutched in her arms and tears rolling down her face. Dad starts toward her, but I get there first and gather her into my arms. She doesn't resist or twist away this time. Instead, she flings her arms around my neck and holds on.

"*Stop...fighting,*" she says between sobs.

Without glancing back at my father, I carry her to our bedroom where I tuck her into the bottom bunk. Then I climb in next to her, stroking her hair until she settles, just like Mom used to do for her—and for me too, when I was her age.

"Izzie?"

I swallow past the lump in my throat. "Yeah?"

"I think our vacation should be over soon. I want to go home."

My resolve grows and sharpens. By the time she's asleep, I'm more convinced than ever about what needs to happen next.

If Dad isn't going to take us home, then I'll have to find a way to get us there myself.

Chapter Twenty-four

No one answers the door at Dane's cabin the next morning. After a minute or two, I take April's hand and start walking toward the lodge, ignoring the nods and good-mornings of the handful of people we pass along the way.

"What are we doing?" April asks, half-running to keep up with me.

"Looking for Dane." Just as I say his name, I spot him in the parking lot, loading a large tote into the Winnebago. The sight of him sparks something in my brain, a memory— his hands gripping the wheel of his parents' Volkswagen as we drove away from the grocery store, the road wide open ahead of us.

Our door is always open for you, my godmother Traci said in our last phone call, shortly before we left for the ranch. In all the chaos and uncertainty of the past couple of weeks, I'd almost forgotten that she lives just three hundred miles south of here. Only half a day's drive...if I can convince someone to take us there.

"Hey," Dane says when he sees me. "I was just about to come looking for you. We're leaving for the campground soon, and I wanted to...." His voice trails off when I move closer, and he sees my frantic expression. "What is it?"

Before I can answer, Kiana sticks her head out from the Winnebago. "Oh. Hi, girls." She takes in the scene—me standing in front of Dane, a look of desperation no doubt plastered all over my face, while April whines and tries to detach herself from my tight grip. "Hey, April," she says cheerfully. "Want to help me get Winnie here ready for the road?"

I let go of her hand, and she heads toward the RV. Once she's inside, I lead Dane to the edge of the parking lot, stopping near a dusty pickup.

I keep my voice low even though there's no one within hearing distance. "How do you feel about another road trip?"

"What?"

"I hate that I'm asking you to do this, but there's literally no one else."

His forehead creases. "What are you asking me to do?"

I glance around us. Dad rarely leaves the construction site before lunch, but I'm still hyperaware of every sound. "April and I need a drive to Stanfield."

"Stanfield? Isn't that like a four-hour drive from here?"

"Five." Someone is walking toward us—it's the tall blond guy who greeted us at the archway the night we got here. I watch him, muscles tense, but he turns and heads toward the main lodge. I wait until he's inside before I turn back to Dane. "My godmother lives there. I have to go see her."

"Why?" he asks, thoroughly confused. "Is she sick or something? Can't your father—"

"My father doesn't know we're going," I explain quickly. "And he can't know, either."

"Isobel, what...?" He shakes his head. "Are you telling me you're running away? And you want me to help you do it?"

I nod, my eyes fastened on his. "After we got back to the cabin last night, Dad and I had a huge fight. He's determined to keep us here, and I can't let that happen. Traci is like family; she said I can go to her if I ever needed help."

"Are you sure about this?" Dane asks me seriously.

"I have to get out of here. I can't even trust what my father says anymore. He said one extra week, then he bought a membership. Now that he's secured us our spots in this place, it doesn't make sense for us to go home anymore. He wants to move us here, and I just—" Panic blazes through me, making me dizzy. "I can't. I hate it here, Dane. I don't want anything to do with this place."

"But your father...."

"He won't *listen* to me," I say, desperation clawing at my stomach. "He's put so much time and hope into this ranch. He's so sure it's the answer for us. He's not going to give up. I'm worried that the longer we stay here, the harder it'll be for him to leave." I take his hand, squeezing it. "Please try to understand."

Dane searches my gaze for a long moment, then he looks away and scratches his jaw, deep in thought. When he turns back to me, he's frowning. "I don't know if I feel comfortable with this."

My heart sinks. If he doesn't agree to help me, we're stuck here. "Please, Dane. There's no bus from here to Stanfield. A taxi would cost way more than I have. No one else here will help me. I'm trapped in this place, and unless I find a way out of it, I'm going to end up stuck here until college."

And what about April? Eventually, she's going to figure out what this ranch is. Is that how I want her to grow up?

Spending weekends here, going through survival training and learning about all the horrible ways the world as we know it might end?

Of course I don't want that. Our father wouldn't either, if he could actually think about it clearly. But he isn't, so it's up to me to make sure that particular future doesn't happen for her. We have little control over the end of the world, but we can control how we live in the meantime.

An idea strikes me, and I squeeze Dane's hand again. "She can vaccinate you. Traci's a pediatric nurse."

He stares at me for a moment, not saying anything. He still looks unsure, but there's a flicker in his eyes. "Without my parents' consent?" he asks doubtfully.

I nod, even though I have no idea whether Traci would stick needles in his arms without clearing it with his moms first. But it's the last card I have to play.

"It's one of the battles you chose, right?" I ask. When he nods, I add, "Well, this is one of mine. I need to get out of here. If I stay, I'm giving in."

He stares at me for another few seconds, then his expression softens, and he lets out a sigh. "When do you want to leave?"

My body lightens. "As soon as possible?"

He glances back at the Winnebago. "I need to help my moms get us set up at the campsite, so it'll have to be tomorrow. I'll come back after dinner tonight, and we can work out a plan, okay?"

"Okay," I say. "And Dane?"

He looks at me, his expression slightly wary.

"Thank you."

The wariness fades, and a smile lights his face. He nods once, and for the first time since we left home, I feel like I can finally breathe.

We decide to leave our bug-out bags behind.

"But what if we have to evacuate?" April asks, saying the last word slowly. She's sitting on the top bunk, watching as I remove piles of clothes from the dresser. We're not taking our suitcases, either—too conspicuous—so I have to figure out some way to stuff everything we need into our backpacks.

"We won't," I say, my hands shaking slightly as I pull open another drawer. I still can't believe we're actually doing this. No, I can't believe it's *come* to this.

It almost didn't happen. By the time Dane returned to the ranch last night, I'd already chickened out about ten times. But then Dad came home early and grilled burgers for dinner, all the while pretending that everything was normal and fine and our fight the night before never happened. I realized nothing is going to change unless I change it myself. His mind is set, and there's nothing I can say to convince him otherwise.

So I didn't feel all that guilty later as Dane and I sat in the guard tower, watching the sunset and forming a plan. We decided to keep it simple. He'd tell his parents the truth, mostly—that he was driving me to my godmother's house and would return the next day, though he'd leave out the part about it being more of an escape mission than a visit. And I'd tell my father that the three of us were spending the day in Holcomb, which has a movie theater and a strip mall and other signs of civilization. Dane's moms aren't at the ranch anymore, so there's no chance of them comparing stories with my dad. I fed April the same white lie, but only because I was worried she might let something slip if I told her the truth.

Now, though, with our father gone for the day and Dane due to pick us up in thirty minutes, I figure it's time to let her in on it.

"April," I say, turning as I stuff several pairs of underwear into each of our bags. "We're not going to Holcomb today. We're going to Traci's."

She moves to the edge of the mattress and swings her legs back and forth in the air. "Oh," she says, unmoved by this vast change in plans. "Is Daddy coming too?"

"No." I watch her face, bracing myself for confusion or questions or even tears. But she just nods and continues to play with Twilight Sparkle, pretending to make her jump over the bunk bed rail like she's a show horse at an eventing competition.

For a moment, I wonder if she understands what I'm actually saying, but then I realize it has nothing to do with comprehension. She just trusts me. I'm her big sister, and as far as she's concerned, big sisters always do the right thing.

Guilt wriggles in my stomach again, but I push it down and continue packing. We're running low on time.

At nine on the dot, April and I head to the parking lot by the lodge, where Dane and I agreed to meet. I hold my breath as we walk, terrified that Dad will appear, notice our overstuffed backpacks, and get suspicious. But the ranch is practically deserted this morning, and no one but a trio of curious squirrels is there to witness our escape. I don't resume breathing again until I see the red Volkswagen, parked in the lot as promised. Dane stands outside of it, rifling through the open trunk. He looks up at the sound of our footsteps on the gravel.

"Hey," he greets us, smiling. As usual, in his T-shirt and board shorts and sunglasses, he looks like he's bound for a day at the beach instead of a secret, impromptu road trip to a stranger's house.

April, clad in her pink-framed sunglasses, grins back at him and skips up to the car. She wiggles out of her backpack and drops it in the trunk, making sure to rescue Twilight Sparkle from the front pocket first.

"You sure you want to do this?" Dane asks me quietly as I place my bag in the trunk next to April's.

I look up at him, seeing my pale image reflected in his sunglasses. "Yes. Are you?"

He shuts the trunk and glances around the quiet ranch like he's seeing it for the last time, even though—unlike April and me—he'll certainly return. "Yeah, I'm sure," he says, his gaze back on me.

Guilt twists through me again, this time because I feel bad for asking so much of him. This is more than just a favor for a friend. He stretched the truth about our trip to his parents. He's helping me outright lie to mine. He's driving six hundred miles round trip on the vague promise that he might get something he wants in return. All for a girl he met a few weeks ago and may never see again.

Am I using him? Does *he* think I am? I don't know, and I don't have time to figure it out now. It's time to go.

I don't look back as we drive under the wooden arch and away from Endurance Ranch. I don't need to. Everything important—well, almost everything—is in this car with me right now.

Chapter Twenty-five

For the first couple hundred miles, Dane keeps me distracted. We talk about music, food, TV shows we both like. I tell him about my mom's *Grey's Anatomy* obsession and how she named April and me after fictional surgeons.

"I think you got off pretty easy," he says. "My grandmother wanted my mother to name me Bane."

I raise my eyebrows. "As in 'the bane of my existence'?"

"Exactly. That's why she didn't want to call me that, even though my grandmother claimed it was a good Hawaiian name. Mom wanted to call me Daniel, so they compromised and settled on Dane, even though I've never set foot in Denmark."

I laugh, my body relaxing for the first time in days. Then his phone's GPS tracking pipes up, its monotone voice telling us to take the next exit, and I tense up again. In a few minutes, we'll hop onto another highway, which will take us all the way to Stanfield and whatever comes afterward.

My stomach lurches, and I glance back at April. She's watching a movie on her tablet and nibbling a granola bar, seemingly unfazed. Then again, our trip to the ranch took days—she's an old pro at long, boring hours in the car. As for me, I feel just as anxious driving away from the ranch as I did driving toward it, though for entirely different reasons.

I picture my father again and his look of terror when he realizes we left. The same look he had when April went missing. It makes my stomach hurt even more, so I push it from my mind and turn back to Dane instead.

"Your moms were really okay with you driving me all this way?" I ask.

"Not entirely. But they know how much I—" He stops talking and clears his throat. "They're okay with it," he says, his cheekbones stained with pink.

My skin warms too. Was he about to say *But they know how much I like you?* Maybe not. Then again, why else would he be willing to do all this for me?

"Dane," I say, fiddling with the pewter charm on my bracelet. "You know I'm never going back there, right? That's why I need to go and see Traci—so she can help me convince Dad that April and I belong at home." I peek at April, but she's still engrossed in her movie, headphones covering her ears. "We might not see each other again after this."

He nods, eyes straight ahead. "I know."

"It's not that I don't...I mean, I really appreciate—"

"I know," he says again, tossing me a quick smile.

Thankfully, the GPS chooses this moment to remind us of our exit, which is looming just ahead. Dane slows down, and we swerve onto the exit ramp. No turning back now.

"You told your godmother about me driving you, right?" he asks once we're settled on the new, multi-lane highway. "She's okay with me crashing there tonight?"

I shift in my seat. "Um, I *will* tell her. When I call her. I'm sure she'll be fine with it."

He glances at me, his dark eyebrows rising above the edge of his sunglasses. "You haven't called her yet?"

"I *couldn't*, Dane," I say, throwing another quick glance to the back seat. "If I told her April and I were coming to visit without Dad, she might have called him and tipped him off. I didn't want to take any chances."

"But...." He tightens his grip on the wheel as a large pickup truck zooms past us on the left. "Are we just going to show up at their door and surprise them? What if they're on vacation or something?"

"They're not. Traci posts everything on Facebook; I'd know if she was. And I *am* going to call," I add, looking at the little arrow—us—on the map, "once we have a long enough head start."

Dane shakes his head. "This feels sketchy."

"Do you want to go back?" I ask, even though I have no idea what we'll do if he says yes. "We could pull off at the next exit and turn around. I don't want to force you to do something you don't feel comfortable with. I'll figure out a way to get to Traci's somehow."

"You're not forcing me. I *want* to help. It's just...." He taps his fingers on the wheel. "I'm worried this will cause even more problems between you and your dad."

"I'll deal with that once we're back home again."

He doesn't say anything to this, and neither of us speaks for several miles. I watch him out of the corner of my eye as he drives, his gaze never straying from the road. I almost ask him if he regrets ever getting involved with me, but I'm afraid to hear the answer.

"You miss it that much, huh?" he says, glancing at me again. "Home?"

The word presses down on me, making my chest throb. "I've been in the same town my entire life. Went to school with all the same kids since elementary. Lived in the same house since I was three years old. April grew up there, took her first steps in the backyard. And my mom...." I swallow and stare at my lap. "I see my mom everywhere there. Kind of hard to leave all that behind, you know?"

Dane reaches across the center console and takes my hand, his warm fingers tight around mine. He might not understand why I'm running, but having him beside me makes the path ahead feel a little less scary.

At around one, we duck into a little town just off the highway and grab lunch at a sandwich place. After we've all eaten and used the bathroom, I ask Dane to watch April for a minute and walk ahead of them outside. I go around to the side of the building to call Traci.

The phone rings and rings. Just as I'm preparing myself to leave a message on her voicemail, the ringing stops, and there she is.

"Hey, sweets, what's up?"

Tears pool in my eyes. I didn't realize exactly how much emotion I had balled up inside of me until I heard her voice. I take a breath and jump in. "Traci? Remember when you made me promise to call you if I ever needed anything? And that your door is always open for me?"

Hearing the strain in my voice, she pauses. "Of course I do, and I meant it too."

I touch Mom's bracelet again, my finger tracing the six letters I know by heart. When I was little, Traci was the only person my mother trusted to take care of me when she and Dad were away. And even though I'm not little anymore, and my mother is gone for good, I still think she'd consider her best friend to be the next best thing to her.

"Good," I say, "because I'm about to take you up on it."

Chapter Twenty-six

We roll into Stanfield just before dinnertime, the GPS guiding us down a tree-lined street to Traci and Heath's house, a brick bungalow with a detached garage and a neat front lawn. It looks just like it did in the pictures they sent when they first moved in. It feels surreal being here, especially when I remember that my mother had been planning a trip to visit Traci a few weeks before she got sick. A trip she never got to take.

As we're collecting our bags from the trunk, the front door opens and Traci steps outside. She's wearing pink nurse's scrubs and sneakers, her long black hair in a messy pile on top of her head. She walks toward us, her eyes shiny and her arms already lifting for a hug.

"You guys are really here," she says, her voice breaking on the last word.

I drop my backpack, letting her gather me into her arms. She smells just like my mom used to, like hand sanitizer and hospital antiseptic. For a moment, with her arms a tight band around me, I feel like everything might turn out okay.

She lets me go and moves on to April, who hugs her back without hesitation, even though she was four the last time we saw Traci and probably doesn't remember her.

"You look just like your mama, you know that?" Traci says as they separate.

April smiles and nods. She does know that.

"And you must be Dane." Instead of hugging him, Traci clasps his hand between both of hers. "Isobel told me a bit about you on the phone. Thank you for getting her and April here safely."

Dane, looking tired and dazed from a day of driving, nods politely. "No problem."

Traci wipes her eyes and looks us over again. "Heath will be so sad he missed you. My husband is a supply technician for the army," she adds for Dane's benefit. "He's overseas right now."

April shifts her weight from one foot to the other. "I need to use the bathroom."

"Oh! Of course." Traci turns and heads back toward the house, motioning for us to follow. "You guys must be hungry too. I just got off work a half hour ago, or else I would've cooked something for dinner. I figure we'll just order some pizza." She puts her arm around my shoulders and directs her next sentence to me alone. "And after dinner, we'll talk."

I nod. On the phone earlier, I'd just told her the basics. All Traci cared about was that we were safe, and everything else could wait until we got here.

Inside, Traci shows April to the bathroom and then takes out her phone to order the pizza. She wanders down the hallway, leaving Dane and me standing in the warm, tidy kitchen. The house is bigger than it looks from outside, and more modern, with its open floor plan and sleek hardwood floors. I see touches of Traci everywhere—in the row of blooming herbs on the windowsill, in the colorful knitted pillows piled on the sofa in the living room across from us. Traci and I are alike that way—we prefer to keep our hands busy.

Dane's phone beeps. He slides it out of his pocket, then types for a few seconds. "My mom," he says. "She wanted to know if we got here okay."

I think about my dad again, who's surely gone back to our cabin by now and discovered us missing. My phone's been on silent since I called Traci hours ago, and I'm afraid to check it.

"You okay?" Dane asks, taking my hand.

I let out a shaky breath. Even though we're here now, safe, my adrenaline is pumping like we're still on the run. "I think so. Are you?"

"Yeah. Just tired." He rubs his eyes and sighs. "It's been a really long day."

April comes into the kitchen then, followed closely by Traci, who has exchanged her scrubs for shorts and a T-shirt. She smiles at Dane and me, her gaze flicking from our faces to our still-linked hands. I didn't tell her *that* particular detail over the phone, either.

"Pizza will be here in twenty," she announces without missing a beat. "In the meantime, make yourselves at home."

After dinner, I get April set up in the living room with her toys, the Disney channel, and the promise that I'll be in the kitchen where she can see me. All day, I've been trying to pretend everything is normal, but she senses something is up. She clung to me all through dinner and only ate a few bites of cheese pizza, even though it's her favorite. For now, though, she seems content to cuddle her crocodile and zone out in front of the TV.

Back in the kitchen, Traci is brewing a pot of chai. I recognize the spicy cinnamon scent; she used to make it every evening when she stayed with us after Mom died. When Traci and Heath heard the news, they hopped on a plane and stayed at our house for two weeks. I'm not sure how we would have managed without them there, feeding us and cleaning the house and doing whatever else needed to be done. I'm not sure how Traci managed it either, as sad as she was over losing her best friend.

"Now," she says, pouring tea into three mugs. She places one in front of each of us and then looks across the table at Dane and me. "Before we do anything else, I think you need to call your father, Isobel."

I freeze with my hand wrapped around the burning cup. "Not yet. I'm not ready to talk to him." More like, I'm not ready for the blast of guilt and anger he's going to fire at me for running away to Traci's.

"Isobel," she says, her brown eyes filled with sympathy. "I don't know what went on between you two, but I do know that punishing him like this isn't going to solve anything. He's worried sick about you and April."

"I didn't leave to punish him." Then I wind back what she just said. *He's worried sick.* "Wait. You called him?"

She blows on her tea and takes a sip. "Of course I did. I called him right after I hung up with you. I wasn't comfortable with him not knowing where you guys were headed. He's your father—he deserves to know where his children are."

The slice of pizza suddenly feels like a lump of granite in my stomach. I glance over at Dane, who's giving me the same sympathetic look as Traci. Under the table, I feel his knee press against mine. "Was he...what did he say? Is he mad?"

"He's worried. He wanted to hop in his car and drive straight here, but I managed to convince him to wait a few hours and get some sleep first. He should be here tomorrow around noon."

My body fills with dread at the thought of facing him. "I'm not going back to that ranch," I say, my spine straight against the back of the chair. "You don't understand, Traci. The people there...."

She folds her arms on the table and leans forward. "Tell me about it, then. Help me understand."

That's all the prompting I need. I tell her everything that happened in the past few months, starting with Dad's descent into prepper mania and ending with April running off to hide in the horse stables. When I'm done, she reaches across the table for my hand, her expression soft and a little bit sad. She gets it now.

"Isobel," she says, squeezing my fingers. "Why didn't you tell me what was happening when I called you weeks ago?"

I take a sip of tea, the warmth and spiciness soothing my dry throat. "I didn't know how bad it was going to get. I thought Dad would listen, that he cared about what I thought, but he doesn't. I guess that's why I'm here now. I didn't know what else to do."

"He does care about you, sweets, so much that he probably doesn't think straight sometimes. I wish it hadn't gotten this bad, but I'm glad you decided to talk to me now. You shouldn't have to deal with this stuff alone. I promised your mom when she was sick that I'd always be there for her girls, and I meant it." She lets go of my hand and looks at Dane, who's mostly been quiet through the entire conversation. "What about you, hon?" she asks him. "How do you feel about all this?"

Dane leans back in his chair. "Actually...." His voice trails off, and he looks at me, unsure.

"What is it?" Traci asks, her gaze bouncing between his face and mine.

Dane starts to say something, then falters, like he's embarrassed to be asking. Or maybe he's afraid—of what his parents will say if they find out, or of the idea itself, I'm not sure. But he didn't drive us all the way here just to go back with nothing. I squeeze his hand, and he takes a deep breath and tries again.

"I want to get vaccinated," he tells Traci. "Isobel said you might be able to do it."

Her eyebrows shoot up. Clearly, she wasn't expecting this. "You're not vaccinated? Against anything?"

He shakes his head. "My parents don't believe in it."

Traci tries to keep her face neutral and professional, like a nurse is taught to do, but I can tell by the slight thinning of her lips that she has a lot of opinions about anti-vaxxers like Dane's parents. "Have you told them you want to be vaccinated?"

"Yeah, but they said they won't give me consent. They think vaccines are toxic and that it's better to build your immunity naturally."

Traci clears her throat and takes a long gulp of her tea, which has to be cold by now. "What are you, seventeen?"

Dane nods.

"Well, in some places, you *do* need parental consent if you're under eighteen. But you're what we'd call a 'mature minor,' which means you're mature enough to understand the risks and benefits of vaccinations." She puts her cup down and meets his eyes. "That means you can give your own consent."

"But my parents told me I couldn't," Dane says, frowning. "Not until I was eighteen."

"They have the wrong information," Traci says gently. "Or maybe they're just giving *you* the wrong information. I don't know. The point is, you can make your own decisions when it comes to your health, Dane. Even if your parents disagree."

Dane stares down at the table for a moment, his jaw twitching and his cheeks flushed red. Then, without looking at either of us, he stands up and leaves the kitchen, disappearing down the hallway before I even have a chance to react. A few seconds later, the sound of the bathroom door closing filters into the kitchen. I look back at Traci, unsure what to do.

"I'm not a parent," she says, "but I deal with them every day. Even the best ones screw up sometimes, Isobel. They do what they believe is right even when people keep telling them they're wrong. They think they're protecting their kids, but all they're really doing is hurting them instead."

Like my dad, pinning all his hopes on a survival community to keep his family safe. All he wants is to protect us, but like Dane's parents—like a lot of parents—he doesn't seem to realize that what he's doing is actually hurting more than it's helping, when it should be the other way around.

I head to the bathroom and knock lightly on the door. It opens immediately, and Dane steps out, avoiding my gaze.

"Are you okay?" I ask, touching his arm.

"Yeah. Sorry I bolted like that. It's just...." He looks at me, his eyes red-rimmed. "I can't believe they lied to me. I always thought...." He shakes his head, letting the sentence trail off, but he doesn't need to say more. I get what it's like when something you always thought you knew turns out to be dead wrong.

Chapter Twenty-seven

When April and I venture out of the guest room the next morning, we find Traci sitting alone at the table, drinking coffee and looking at her phone. I glance around for Dane, but the bed Traci set up on the couch for him is empty and he's nowhere to be seen.

"He got up early and went to the doctor," Traci answers my unasked question. "A friend of mine works at a walk-in clinic in town, so I sent him there. They'll start his vaccination series no problem. I would've brought him into the hospital and done it myself, but he said he needed to take care of this on his own."

I sit down in the chair across from her and pull April down on my lap. "Thanks, Traci."

She smiles. "Anytime, sweets."

By the time April and I eat breakfast and shower, Dane is back from the doctor, looking tired and slightly pale. Traci immediately makes him sit down on the couch and rest.

"Just for an hour," she tells him when he insists that he feels fine. "To make sure you don't have any adverse reactions."

She catches my eye before she leaves the room, taking April with her, and I realize what she's really doing. She's giving me a bit of extra time with him before he leaves to go back to his parents.

"Are you really okay?" I ask, sitting beside him on the couch.

"I'm fine," he says again. "Just sore, that's all. But I'm glad I did it."

I run my finger lightly over the Band-Aid on his upper arm. "Me too."

He leans back against the pile of knitted pillows and takes my hand. "So," he says, glancing at me, "I guess your dad will be here soon."

"Yeah," I say, biting my lip. "He's probably going to kill me."

"Well, my moms are probably going kill me too once they find out I've been pumped full of vaccines." He laughs. "Which would kind of defeat the purpose, I guess."

I lean my head against his shoulder, careful not to press on his sore arm, and laugh with him. We stay like that for a while, not talking, listening to the ticking wall clock above us and Traci's cheerful voice as she tries to distract April in the kitchen. Each hour felt like days when we were driving here yesterday, but now, sixty minutes feels nowhere near long enough.

"You know," Dane says, lacing his fingers with mine, "I did a lot of thinking when we were staying at the ranch, and I realized some things about myself that I never really considered before. Like sometimes, I go along with my moms just because it's easier than going against them. When they told me I couldn't get immunized without their consent, I just assumed they were telling me the truth, so I let it go. I never thought about going to the doctor and finding out for myself." He tips his head back against the couch. "You were right before. I *am* too passive."

I pull back to look at him. "Seriously? Voluntarily getting jabbed with sharp needles to protect yourself against horrible life-threatening diseases sounds like the opposite of passive to me."

He blinks and laughs. "I think I was right about you too. You *are* always this blunt."

"I'm trying to be."

Dane's smile fades. "I'm sorry I won't be here when your dad gets here."

I press close to him again. "You have to get back to your moms, huh?" I say into his chest.

"I promised I'd be back before dinner," he says, wrapping his arm around me.

"It's okay," I say. "It's better that you're not here when he arrives." All of this had been my decision, and I didn't want Dane to get caught in the cross fire.

Traci walks in then, some kind of small gadget in her hand. "Sorry for interrupting. Just wanted to check you over, Dane."

The gadget turns out to be a digital thermometer, which she points at Dane's forehead. Seconds later, it beeps out a reading.

"Perfect," Traci announces. Next, she checks under his Band-Aid for swelling, then feels his pulse. Finally, she tells him he's good to go. "Keep your vaccine schedule safe and don't forget to make an appointment with a doctor when it's time for another dose."

"I won't forget," he says, standing up. "Thanks for everything."

Traci gives him a quick hug. "Take care of yourself."

He nods and heads toward April. "Bye, April."

She flings her arms around his waist. "Bye, Dane."

My heart lodged somewhere in the back of my throat, I walk with him outside to the Volkswagen. He tosses his bag in the back seat and then turns to me, pulling me against his chest. I wrap my arms around him and press my lips to his, trying to pour all my feelings and gratitude into this one last kiss.

"Thank you for being there for me," I say, pulling back and resting my chin against his shoulder. "Spending time with you was the only thing that kept me sane these past few weeks. I just...I wish...."

His arms tighten around me. "I know. Me too." We stand like that for a few moments, neither of us wanting to let go. "We can text," he says quietly. "And call."

"Okay," I say, even though I know it won't be the same. It won't be like this ever again.

We let each other go and I step back, watching as he gets into the car. He doesn't look at me again until his sunglasses are in place and the engine is running.

"Bye, Isobel," he says through the open window. Then he backs up and drives away.

I stand there on the damp pavement, my chest aching with each breath. Finally, I turn around and go back inside. Traci is in the living room, stripping the bedding off the couch.

"Oh, sweetheart," she says when she sees my wet, puffy face. She drops the blanket she's folding and comes over to hug me. "That's a nice young man you have there."

"I know," I say, even though as of this moment, I no longer have him at all.

"Are we going home today, Izzie?"

I look over at April, who's helping me tidy up Traci's guest room. "I don't know," I say, tossing her crocodile to the foot of the bed so I can tuck in the sheets. "We'll have to wait until Dad gets here."

She sighs and flops back on the smooth comforter, arms crossed tightly over her chest. She hasn't been herself since the night she ran off to the stables. The sooner we get back home to our normal lives, the better.

I grab the croc and press his snout to her cheek, making a loud kissing noise. "Love you."

Her lips twitch into a tiny smile. "Love you too."

The doorbell rings then, followed by voices. One of them is Traci's, and the other is deeper and distinctly familiar. My heart thumps in my chest.

"Daddy!" April cries, bolting off the bed and out the bedroom door.

I finish making the bed, moving slowly to give my pulse some time to slow down before I have to face him. I edge my way out of the bedroom and down the hallway, stopping at the threshold to the living room. My father is standing in the middle of the room, April wrapped around his torso like a baby koala. He meets my eyes over the top of her head. The mixture of relief and anger on his face makes my stomach drop.

"Isobel," he says, disappointment stuffed into each syllable. He puts April down and comes over to hug me, taking me off guard for a moment. The he pulls back to look at me, his bloodshot eyes simmering with anger again. "You had me worried *sick*. How could you just leave like that, especially after what we just went through with April? And getting Dane involved in it too? What were you *thinking*?"

My own anger bubbles in my throat like acid. "I was *thinking* I didn't want to spend the rest of my life preparing for the end of the world."

"That's no excuse to take your sister on some road trip like—"

I cross my arms. "Like you did with us?"

There's a beat of silence as we stare at each other, weeks of built-up hurt passing between us. I try to take a deep breath and steady myself, but my chest feels tight and constricted.

"Get your things," he says tightly.

Traci steps forward. "Gabe...."

Dad tosses her a glance, his face red. "I appreciate everything you've done, Traci, but this is between me and my girls."

"No," I say, my heart thumping double-time. "I'm not going back to the ranch, and neither is April. Russell probably doesn't even want us there, and Nick definitely doesn't. He thinks I'm a security threat."

"Don't be ridiculous, Isobel."

"It's true. I told you how he overheard me mentioning the ranch to some random lady in the hardware store. He grabbed my arm and practically told me to keep my mouth shut." I swallow hard, remembering his clammy fingers on my skin. "What if it's not me who slips up next time? What if it's April? What if Nick does the same thing to her?"

He shakes his head like he doesn't want to hear it and holds his hand out to April. "Come on, Sunshine. Let's get your bags."

"So that's it?" My breath catches in my throat. "Nothing I say matters?"

April glances at me, unsure, before moving closer to Dad and taking his hand. He starts toward the bedroom, but I slip in front of him, blocking his way.

"You used to listen to me, Dad. You used to make me feel so safe and protected. But I don't feel that way anymore. The ranch doesn't make me feel safe—it makes me feel like I can't breathe. Don't you understand? I can't...."

A wave of dizziness washes over me, making my legs weak, and I stumble. My vision turns fuzzy and then everything goes dark.

The next thing I know I'm lying down and Traci's fingers are pressed against my wrist. "She hyperventilated and blacked out," she says, her voice like a faraway echo even though I can feel her right next to me. "Breathe slowly, Isobel."

I try. My vision clears, and I glance over at Dad, still standing at the threshold to the living room, his face white and stony. April crouches beside Traci, watching me, her eyes wide with fear.

"What's wrong, Izzie?" she asks, her little fingers gripping my arm. "Are you sick? Are you going to die?"

Speaking seems like too much effort, so I just pat her curls to reassure her. Seeing how scared she is, how conditioned she's become to assume the worst-case scenario, dissolves some of the fog in my head. I sit up slowly and take a deep, even breath.

"I'll be okay," I say, because clearly I'm not okay right now—none of us are.

"Now," Traci says, sitting beside me and gripping my trembling hand. "How about we all talk this through calmly? You've clearly suffered a communication breakdown, and seeing as you're all currently in my house, I'd like to help you guys through it. Because what you've been doing obviously isn't working."

I look at April, guilt slicing through me when I notice the tears on her face. She doesn't need to hear any more yelling. But we've been at odds for so long, and so much has happened, I'm not sure how we're going to be able to sit down for a calm, productive conversation.

But for April, I'm willing to try. I stay put on the couch next to Traci, and April—encouraged by the attempt at civility—goes over and takes Dad's hand, leading him to the chair opposite us. He sits down slowly, as if still in shock, and April joins Traci and me on the couch.

"Now, Gabe," Traci begins, her voice gentle again. "I get why you're upset. What Isobel did was wrong—she shouldn't have left without telling you. But after hearing what she had to say about this ranch and how far you've gotten into the doomsday prepping...I think you need to consider the fact that a lot of this is actually stemming from your anxiety disorder."

Confused, I turn to look at her. *Anxiety disorder?*

"You're a pediatric nurse, Traci," Dad says gruffly, "not a psychiatric one."

She ignores his tone and leans forward, her gaze soft but direct, like Traci herself. "Gabe. This has been happening for years now, and it's gotten worse. Lisa spoke to me about it many times. She was worried about you then, and I bet your girls are worried about you now. You thought you were fine, but I'm not sure you are. And I don't think you're sure either."

April snuggles into me, but I barely register the solid weight of her against my arm. An anxiety disorder that's been going on for years. How had I missed it? How had they kept it hidden from me? I mean, I've always known my father was anxious—all the check-in texts, hiding inside from storms—but I thought it had to do with the state of the world, which even I can admit is scary.

Dad stares at her, his jaw set. "I don't want to discuss this right now."

"Then *when*, Gabe?" Traci says, a slight tremor in her voice. "One of Lisa's biggest worries when she was sick was how you'd cope if she died. She was terrified that without her there to center you, you'd let your anxiety take over and it would end up affecting the girls." She pauses to glance at April and me. "And she was right. Look at them, Gabe. Look what this is doing to your girls."

Dad looks at us, huddled together on the couch, April crying and me still shaky and probably white as a sheet. Something in him shifts. He leans forward, elbows resting on his knees and his gaze focused on the floor. For a moment, the only sounds in the room are the ticking of the clock and his long, measured breaths.

"You need to get help, Gabe," Traci says softly. "For your daughters, for yourself, and for Lisa too. So you can be the kind of parent she needed you to be."

To my horror and amazement, he starts to cry. I haven't seen him weep like this since the day Mom died, when he stood over her body and stroked her bare scalp where her curls used to be. Those tears came from loss, from love, from the crushing awareness that the world as we knew it was gone forever. Maybe it's the same this time, or maybe he finally realized that he's been preparing us for the end more than he's been living with us in the *now*—with whatever time we have left to enjoy—and that's what would bother Mom most of all.

"Daddy!" Panicked again, April jumps up and goes to him, throwing her arms around his heaving shoulders. "Don't cry, Daddy," she whispers. "Let's just go home, okay? Then everything will be better. Okay, Daddy? I really want to go home."

Dad pulls her onto his lap and presses his cheek against her hair. Then he looks up at me, his eyes red and pleading, and I don't even hesitate. I go to him too, gripping his hand as he whispers *I'm sorry* over and over again through his tears.

Chapter Twenty-eight

Later, after Traci convinces us to stay for the night, she takes April outside to check out her vegetable garden, leaving Dad and me alone in the kitchen. He fills two glasses with water at the sink then hands one to me, his bloodshot eyes steady on mine. He looks about as drained as I feel, but the air is definitely lighter between us. Still, there's the unspoken question of what happens when we leave here tomorrow.

"I have to go back to the ranch in the morning," Dad says.

For a moment, that hard-won lightness disappears, and I feel my body lock up.

He places his glass on the counter. "No, *you* don't have to go back to the ranch. I do. I need to pick up the rest of our things." He leans against the counter. "It's all arranged. I'm going to drop you girls off with Kiana and Charlene at the campground they're staying at and then go back to the ranch myself."

Dane, I get to see Dane again. But the thought quickly dissipates as I struggle to grasp the rest. "Wait. What does this mean?"

"We're leaving," he says. "I'm selling back our member-ships and we're leaving the ranch."

I just stare at him, my mind spinning. "But what's Russell going to say? And Dennis? You think they're going to be okay with you changing your mind?"

He shrugs. "They're going to have to be okay with it. What you said about Nick before...I should have taken it more seri-ously, but I couldn't see past my own anxiety and paranoia."

"I just thought you didn't believe me."

"Tater," Dad says, and for a moment I think he's go-ing to start crying again. "I'm so sorry. I think I just didn't *want* to believe you. I wanted so badly for that place to help us, to finally make *me* feel safe, and I thought once you got used to it, you'd feel safe there too. I didn't listen to you about Nick or any of it. It wasn't until I saw you on that couch, looking so...God. And when April asked if you were going to die...." He sighs and runs a hand over his tired face. "I'm sorry it took me so long to realize what this has been doing to you both."

Tears fill my eyes. I've been waiting so long to hear that from him.

"Things have been pretty rough between us since your mom died, haven't they?" he says, reaching up to gently wipe my cheek. "I still don't know how to process it. Even when she was at her sickest and the doctors said there was noth-ing more they could do, I couldn't believe she wouldn't al-ways be here. I never let myself believe she might not make it. Maybe if I had, I would have been more prepared."

I nod, my throat tight. I'd thought she'd always be here too, fluttering around our kitchen and singing off-key and making us laugh with her stories. I wasn't prepared either. How can anyone be prepared for a loss so huge that it shifts the ground beneath your feet and alters you forever?

"Traci's right," he goes on. "I need to get some help managing all of this, for myself and for you and April, and I can't do that if I'm surrounded by people who feed into all my fears."

Hope ignites in my chest, making my next breath come easy. This can only mean one thing. "So…we're going home?"

He just looks at me, assessing, but not in the calculating way like he's examining a threat. More like he's just seeing *me*, his daughter. And for a moment I can almost see the old Dad, the Dad he was before our family changed shape and the world as we knew it changed too. "We're going home."

"Okay," Traci says once we're assembled by the door with our bags, well-rested and ready to go. "You all have my number, and I expect regular check-ins, at least once a month. Deal?"

Dad leans over to kiss her cheek. "Thanks, Trace."

"You're going to be fine. You have more power than you think, Gabe." She squeezes his arm and then turns to April. "And you, Little Miss," she says, tousling her wild hair. "Be good for your dad and big sister. No more running off into thunderstorms and worrying everyone. Got it?"

She giggles and hops away, skipping down the hall and back again. To my relief, she seemed to bounce right back to her normal self once she was sure that Dad and I were okay again. She never did need much to be happy.

"That girl," Traci says, watching her with a grin. "Her energy never quits, does it? She's like her mom that way.

Lisa could never sit still, remember? Always bustling around, jiggling her leg, tapping her fingers. It drove me kind of mad sometimes."

I think of Mom's fingers keeping the beat on the steering wheel. She was always in motion.

"I sure missed it, though," Traci adds. "After."

Dad nods, his expression softening. "Me too."

We're all quiet for a moment, remembering, until we're interrupted by April crashing into Dad's legs. He smiles and reaches down to steady her. "How about you help me put the bags in the car, Sunshine?"

She grabs her backpack and heads for the door, Dad following behind with our bags and the care package of snacks Traci packed up for us. Once they're outside, Traci turns to me and pulls me in for a hug.

"April may look like your mom, but you have her optimism and strength," she says against my hair. She pulls back to look at me. "Remember, though...even the strongest people need to ask for help sometimes. You can't fix everything by yourself, Isobel."

I nod. She's right—I couldn't fix all the broken pieces left behind when Mom died, but maybe I shouldn't have assumed the responsibility was mine in the first place. And if Dad's willing to work harder to hear me and what I need, then maybe we can start repairing those breaks together.

"Be patient with your dad, sweets," Traci says, giving me another quick hug. "He's made a lot of mistakes, but he's trying."

I nod again, letting her know I'll try too, before moving toward the door. Just as I'm about to go outside, I turn back to Traci again. "Thanks. For everything."

She smiles. "Anytime. It was so nice to have you all here, even if the circumstances weren't ideal."

I place my hand on the doorknob, ready to leave, but then turn back a second time. There's one more thing I want to know before I go. "Remember I told you once that it was my dream to go to Chapman College of Art and Design?"

"Of course I remember," she says without hesitation. "And I told you I'd be happy to have you stay with us if you ended up going there. I meant it, you know. You always have another home here with Heath and me. Don't ever forget that."

After the past couple of weeks, it's hard to imagine a time when I'll ever want to leave home again. But it's comforting to know that if I do find myself back here, it won't be because I'm running away from somewhere else.

"I won't forget," I tell her, then I step outside to join my family.

Chapter Twenty-nine

The five-hour drive seems to take at least five hundred years, probably because we're just one stop away from officially heading east toward home. And because I know that at the end of it, I'll get one more chance to see Dane.

The old Winnebago is the first thing I see as we pull into the campground, which is basically just a big grassy field overlooking a rocky beach. Kiana is out front, hanging a blanket over the backs of two lawn chairs. It rained a lot last night. When she sees us approaching, she turns and leans in the door of the camper. Seconds later, Charlene emerges, followed closely by Dane. He catches my eye and smiles, and my heart somersaults in my chest.

"I'll be back in an hour or so," Dad tells us as he waves to Dane's parents.

I turn to him, suddenly worried. "Be careful, okay?"

Dad nods. "Always."

April and I get out and watch him drive away, the car's tires kicking up a cloud of dust that follows him all the way back to the highway. Once he's gone, I take my sister's hand, and we turn toward the Winnebago, where Dane and his moms are waiting for us.

"Who's in the mood for banana muffins?" Charlene asks. April bounces toward them. "Me!"

I lock eyes with Dane again. The muffins can wait.

Once April is settled at a picnic table with her snack, Dane and I walk around the campground. Even for a sunny day in the middle of July, the place is virtually deserted. That's a good thing though, because when we pause near the horseshoe pit for a kiss, no one sees us but the birds flying around the beach below.

"Thought you were rid of me, huh?" I ask when we pull away.

He laughs and takes my hand as we continue walking. "I hoped I wasn't. So how did it go with your dad? My mom said he was leaving the ranch."

I tell him everything, the words coming out in a rush. I still can't wrap my head around everything that's happened in the past twenty-four hours. "How did it go with your moms?" I ask once I finish. "They didn't kill you, I see. Or did you not tell them you got vaccinated?"

"No, I told them," he says. "They were really mad at first. We fought about it, but I think they realize that I'm entitled to my own opinions and I'm old enough now to make decisions for myself. I think they were more hurt that I went behind their backs, but hey, they lied too."

I nod. Despite their differences in parenting styles, my dad and his moms have more in common than just doomsday prepping.

We linger for a while before heading back to the Winnebago and April. When Dad gets back, I want us to be ready.

"I'm glad I got to see you again," I say as we circle around to the front of the camper. "Because there's something I wanted to give you."

I reach into my purse and pull out the stone pendant that I finished last night in Traci's kitchen, after everyone else was asleep. It's not nestled in tissue paper or a cute little gift bag, like most of the jewelry I give to people, but that's okay. It's the recipient that matters, not the presentation.

"You *made* this?" Dane says, running his thumb over the smooth, polished stone. "It's amazing. Thank you."

He loosens the sliding knots on the nylon cord and slips it over his head. I help him adjust the length so the stone rests perfectly below his collarbone, just like I imagined it would when I sketched out the design the night we kissed for the first time in the guard tower. Even before I started making it, I knew it was meant for him.

"Something to remember me by," I say, straightening the stone on his chest.

"I don't need a reminder. Besides," he adds, smiling, "we might see each other again sooner than you think."

"What do you mean?"

"My moms are reconsidering the ranch too."

I stare at him, shocked. I thought his parents were all over the idea of Endurance Ranch. "Seriously? Why?"

"They're not okay with survival skills that involve guns and violence," he says. "Plus they really don't like Nick."

I snicker. "Who does?"

"It's not only that, though. I'd like to do something on my own for once, maybe travel or go away to college. Who knows? I think I need to figure out who I am apart from all this." He grins and raises an eyebrow. "How's that for the opposite of passive?"

I laugh and press my forehead against his shirt, breathing in his familiar minty scent. Maybe we'll see each other again someday, or maybe we won't. There's no way to know for sure. The future is unpredictable.

But I hope we do.

As promised, Dad returns after an hour, unscathed and loaded down with our bug-out bags and the rest of the things we left behind. I'm aware that nothing short of an actual apocalypse would ever stop him from coming back for us, but I'm still relieved to see him.

We leave shortly after, armed with banana muffins and promises to keep in touch. I wave to Dane one last time as we drive away, then I settle back in my seat, feeling calmer than I have in months. We'll only be on the road for three more hours before stopping for the night, but we're traveling in the right direction and that's all that matters.

"How'd it go at the ranch?" I ask my father once we're settled on the highway. "Was it hard to leave?"

"No." He turns on the stereo, and the car fills with his familiar nineties grunge. "It was surprisingly easy."

I was actually asking about logistics, like how hard it was to get rid of our memberships, but I sense my father is talking about something else altogether. In any case, it's reassuring that no matter how adamant he was about going there, or how much work he put into the new shelter, he's choosing what's best for his family now over the place he believed was our only salvation.

"That was a really nice necklace you made for Dane," Dad says after a while.

I glance up from the novel-sized update text that I'm writing for Claire. Okay, maybe he notices more than I realize. "Thanks."

"You have a lot of talent. I bet you could get into any art school you wanted."

"Well," I begin hesitantly. The last time I tried to discuss this with him, he was too wrapped up in his anxiety to really hear me. But now, he seems relaxed and open. "I've been thinking a lot about Chapman College of Art and Design." I look at my phone again. "It's really far from home, though."

"Chapman College?" he asks.

"Yeah," I say. "Where my art teacher Ms. Sheridan went?" He still looks confused, and I think back to that day. It was just a few weeks ago, though it feels like months. He'd been so scared, listening to the weather on the TV in the dim living room. "Ms. Sheridan thinks I might get in. She said she'd write me a good reference for my application."

He glances in the rearview at April, who's humming as she brushes Twilight Sparkle's hair. "If you want to go there, you should go. We'll miss you wherever you end up, and you'll miss us, but we'll all be okay, right?"

I stare at my dad. I'd forgotten he could be like this, so calm and rational and comforting. It reminds me a little bit of what it was like before. With Mom. I don't think I'd recognized just how much he'd changed.

"Maybe," I reply, trying to imagine it, leaving April for months at a time. Leaving them both. After Mom died, I fell into the role I thought we needed in her absence. I took care of April. I tried—and failed—to keep our father from slipping over the edge. But maybe those roles were never mine to fill. Maybe—now that Dad has agreed to get the help he needs to finally heal and move on—they *could* manage just fine without me. And maybe I can manage just fine without them too.

I hit send on the text to Claire. There's still so much I need to tell her, but the rest can wait until we get home. "Well, Traci *did* say I could stay with them if I ended up at Chapman."

Dad smiles. "Your mom would've loved that idea."

April, always listening, stops humming and says, "Tell me about Mommy."

Her words fill me with warmth. We haven't done Mom Facts in a while. I scour my brain for something I haven't already told her, but before I can come up with anything, Dad speaks first.

"She was brave." His smile softens, like he's recalling a private memory. "And determined. The worse things got, the more she tried to focus on the good."

I touch the bracelet on my wrist, a part of her I'll carry with me always, and rest my forehead against the window. I spot a bird flying above, heading in the same direction, wings spread as she glides along the treetops. Something about it makes me think of the mixed media art project Ms. Sheridan suggested I include in my college application portfolio, the one with the newspaper bird surrounded by feathers and old-fashioned cages. The bird who sits on her painted perch, joyfully singing despite all those cages in the background, a constant reminder of how small her world can get. But for the moment, at least, she's free.

Acknowledgments

I wrote the first draft of *The End of Always* in 2019, a few months before the world turned upside down. Back then, I was like Isobel, completely mystified by doomsday preppers and unwavering in my optimistic view of the world. Now, after living through a pandemic and lockdowns in 2020 and beyond, witnessing Hurricane Fiona's destruction in 2022, and watching my beautiful province burn and then flood in 2023, I understand a little more why someone might go to such lengths to prepare for disaster. But like Isobel says, *Instead of preparing for the end of the world, wouldn't it make more sense to, you know, put all that energy into trying to fix it?* I still believe that.

Thank you to the awesome team at Second Story Press— Jordan Ryder, Margie Wolfe, Phuong Truong, Emma Rodgers, Michaela Stephen, Beatrice Glickman, Kate Earnshaw, April Masongsong, and anyone else behind the scenes who had a hand in bringing *The End of Always* to life.

Many thanks to Erin McCluskey and Laura Atherton for the stunningly perfect cover that I can't stop staring at. You nailed it.

A huge thank you to my amazing editor, Erin Della Mattia, for understanding the story I wanted to tell and then helping me tell it in a much better way. Working with you was a pleasure.

Thank you to Eric Smith, this book's first reader and champion. I appreciate you.

Thank you to my lovely family and friends for the endless support and GIFs. I adore you all. And to my Stretch Creative ladies who happily covered for me while I edited this book.

Lastly, thank you to my wonderful husband and children, whose enduring love, humor, and support has gotten me through every roller-coaster book-writing venture, including this one. Love you always. There's no one else I'd rather share an underground bunker with at the end of the world.

About the Author

Rebecca Phillips is a copyeditor by day and a TV-series-binger by night. Oh, and sometimes she writes novels. Rebecca lives in beautiful Nova Scotia with her family, which includes a spoiled senior-citizen cat.